Pride goeth before the fall. . . .

Was she crazy?

Kaia stared out the dusty window of the pickup truck, wondering if she'd lost her mind. She didn't even know why she'd called him. So he was hot. Fine. There was no point in denying that. Nor could she deny the fact that when he looked at her, when his eyes burned into her, she trembled.

But that was irrelevant. It had to be. Kaia Sellers could *not* involve herself with someone like this *Weed*, poor, stupid, aimless, and completely unacceptable. Couldn't, and wouldn't. And yet . . .

And yet, she'd made the call. And when he'd shown up at her door, she'd welcomed him in, hadn't she? Leaned toward him, so he would smell her perfume. Favored him with a sultry smile.

And now here she was in the old truck, Reed by her side, speeding through the darkened landscape, the lights of civilization (if Grace qualified) fading into the distance behind them.

I must be crazy, Kaia thought, unsure whether to be appalled or amused. It was the only possible explanation.

Crazy was fine—for a night. But whatever happened, Kaia promised herself, one night was all it would ever be.

SEVEN DEADLY SINS

Lust
Envy
Pride

SOON TO BE COMMITTED:
Wrath

SEVEN DEADLY SINS

pride

ROBIN WASSERMAN

SIMON PULSE
New York   London   Toronto   Sydney

〰 SIMON PULSE
An imprint of Simon & Schuster Children's Publishing Division
1230 Avenue of the Americas, New York, NY 10020
Copyright © 2006 by Robin Wasserman
Designed by Ann Zeak
The text of this book was set in Bembo.
Manufactured in the United States of America
First Simon Pulse edition April 2006
10 9 8 7 6 5 4 3 2 1
Library of Congress Control Number 2005933860
ISBN-13: 978-0-689-87784-1
ISBN-10: 0-689-87784-6

For Mom and Dad

He that is proud eats up himself: pride is
his own glass, his own trumpet, his own chronicle.
—William Shakespeare, *Troilus and Cressida*

This world is mine for the taking.
—Eminem

chapter

1

They wanted him. All of them. He knew it.

And he loved it.

Kane Geary had developed many gifts in his eighteen years of life, not least of which was a finely tuned radar for the appreciative stares of beautiful women. And tonight, he could feel their eyes on him, their gazes drawn to him from all over the restaurant. The luscious redhead in the back booth, stealing glances over her date's sloping shoulders; the trim blonde waiting for the bathroom, zeroing in on his chiseled pecs; their perky waitress, shamelessly grazing his shoulder as she leaned across him to lay out their food—even the age-weathered brunette up in front was joining in the fun, catching his eye with a wink every time her balding husband's back was turned.

Seated on the edge of Chez Jacques's spacious dining room, which bustled with the well-bridled enthusiasm of a small-town Saturday night, Kane was, quite simply, the center of attention. Which was exactly how he liked it.

Not that Kane was an attention-grabber, one of those tedious people who talked too much, too fast, too loudly. That would be too obvious. And far too much work. Instead, he waited, knowing that his smoldering good looks and effortless grace would eventually and inevitably draw the world to him. Or, more specifically, draw the girls.

They came in all shapes, colors, and sizes, and they wanted only one thing: him. Which meant that Kane could take his pick. And he usually did.

This time, he thought, smiling at the blond beauty sitting across the table from him, *I may be onto something.* Beth Manning seemed to have it all: brains, personality, body by Barbie . . . and, as of two months ago, she had him.

She was, to put it mildly, an unlikely choice. Haven High's resident most-likely-to-succeed, a power player when it came to AP classes and extracurriculars, a nobody when it came to anything else. Beth was the world's original "nice girl," and Kane knew that, until recently, dating him had never crossed her mind. Nice girls didn't date Kane Geary. They stuck with people like Adam Morgan, Mr. All-American, earnest, good-hearted, and sweet as apple pie. But now Adam was history, and Beth was all his.

All it had taken was a little hard work, just a few surreptitious pushes in the right direction . . . and here she was. Tossed aside by her beloved boyfriend, who'd caught her cheating. With Kane. Or, at least, Adam *thought* he'd caught her. Kane smirked. You'd think that after their years of friendship, Adam would have realized that when it came to Kane, what you see is rarely what you get. But Adam hadn't bothered to look deeper; and Kane hadn't hesitated before swooping in to claim his prize.

And what a prize. Perched primly on the edge of her seat, her hand on his, his foot grazing her leg beneath the table. Gazing at him with those open, grateful eyes—as if a dinner at Chez Jacques, the overpriced "French bistro" whose chef and menu were about as French as McDonald's french fries, was proof of his boundless love. Yes, it was "the best restaurant in town"—but when your town was a dusty assortment of liquor stores and burned-out buildings like Grace, California, and when most local cuisine tasted as if a handful of desert dirt and cacti had been tossed in for "local flavor," best restaurant in town wasn't saying much. Not that Beth seemed to realize it. Kane supposed that a lifetime in Grace—or perhaps a year with Adam—had dulled her expectations. Or at least her tastebuds.

She'd temporarily dispensed with her daily uniform, a bland T-shirt and jeans, and was instead wearing a low-cut satin dress, a pale sky blue that matched her eyes. With her long, blond hair swept into a loose knot at the nape of her neck and the long, silver earrings he'd given her swaying gently with her every graceful move, she looked like a model. Gorgeous, elegant—perfect. And should he expect any less?

Kane could see the question in the envious gazes of his female admirers: What does *she* have that I don't?

One thing, ladies, he responded silently, suppressing a smile. *For the moment—me.*

"What are you thinking?" she asked him, tucking a stray hair behind her ear. It had become a familiar question. Good ol' Adam was pretty much an open book—it must be somewhat unnerving for her, Kane supposed, to be dating someone with any kind of inner life, someone with secrets. And Kane didn't mind her asking—as long as he didn't have to give a real answer.

"I'm just thinking how beautiful you look tonight," Kane told her—a half-truth being the best kind of lie. "I'm thinking how incredibly lucky I am to have ended up with someone like you."

Beth giggled, her face turning a faint shade of pink. "I'm the lucky one, Kane," she protested.

He couldn't argue with that.

For Harper Grace, Saturday night traditionally meant three things: booze, boys, and boredom. She would hit a lame bar with a lame guy, flash her crappy fake ID at an apathetic bartender, and down a couple of rum and Cokes before finding a secluded spot for the inevitable not-so-hot 'n' heavy make-out session with Mr. Wrong. It had seemed a risky and adventurous formula a few years ago, but the love 'm and lose 'em act had gotten old, fast. Grace was a small town, too small—and after a few years of the same bars, the same guys, the same post-date conversation with her best friend, Miranda (usually concluding with, "Why would you ever let me go out with such a loser?"), the thrill was gone.

But, now . . . Harper glanced to her left. Adam's wholesome good looks were just barely visible in the dim light cast by the flickering movie screen. His bright eyes, his wide smile, the shock of blond hair that set off his perfect tan—it was too dark to see the details, but no matter. She knew them all by heart.

Now, things were different, Harper reminded herself, leaning against Adam's broad shoulder and twirling her fingers through his. There was no more need for cheap thrills, because she had the real thing. Adam Morgan, her next-door neighbor, her oldest friend—her soul mate, if you believed in such things. Which, of course, she didn't. But she believed in Adam—and she believed that after all the effort she'd put into winning him, she fully deserved her prize. They'd been together only a couple months, but already, he never spoke of his year with The Bland One anymore. The dreamy gaze that used to bloom across his face at the mere mention of Beth's name was gone. Knowing—or believing—that his perfect little angel had hopped into bed with someone else had had its effect. Adam had finally wised up and realized that the right person for him had been there all along, a loyal friend and next-door neighbor, just waiting for her time to come. Unlike Beth, *Harper* would never let him down, never mistreat him, never lie to him—unless, she conceded, it was for his own good.

So what if she was spending her night in a dark theater watching an endless Jackie Chan marathon rather than preening in front of the adoring masses, Haven High girls hoping that her polite acknowledgment might secure them a berth on the A-list, brawny bouncers and bartenders attracted by her billowing auburn hair like moths to a flame and hoping against hope she would ditch her date and fall into their open arms? (It had been known to happen.) So what if she had to watch what she said 24/7, to make sure none of the nasty thoughts constantly popping into her brain slipped out in Adam's presence, lest he begin to think she really was as much of a power-hungry bitch as the rest of their school believed her to be? And so what if, in order to get what she wanted, she'd had to screw over the people she loved the most, and sacrifice whatever shreds of integrity she may have had left after four years in the Haven High trenches?

None of that mattered now. Not now that she had Adam. Strong, handsome, kind, wonderful, *perfect* Adam.

She'd waited so long—but it had been worth it. All of it.

"What are you thinking?" he whispered, slinging an arm around her and drawing her close. She nestled against him, laying her head against his shoulder. He was always asking her that, and she was still delighted by the novelty of being with a guy who actually cared what she was thinking, who was focused on getting into her mind rather than into her bed.

"I'm thinking this—you, us—it's all too good to be true," she admitted. And though it was intended as a lie, the words had the ring of truth.

"It's true," he assured her, and kissed her gently on the forehead.

I'll reform, Harper decided, leaning against his warm body. No more party girl. No more shallow, superficial bitch. She would be the girl Adam wanted her to be—the girl he seemed to think, deep down, she really was. And who knew? He could even be right.

After all, anything's possible.

Miranda was bored.

She'd tried to tell herself that having all this free time

on her hands was a good thing. She could use some space—a nice, long stretch of empty hours every now and then would give her a chance to do all the things that she wanted to do. She wouldn't have to accommodate anyone else—not her mother, not her little sister, not Harper, none of the people who usually saw fit to dictate the what, when, and how of Miranda's life. She'd just do her own thing. She was a strong, smart, independent woman, right? (This month's *Cosmo* quiz had confirmed it.) Enjoying your alone time was right there in the job description, and she'd been certain she was up to the task.

But it was time to face facts. These last few weeks she'd read plenty of good books, watched all her favorite movies, taken so many "relaxing" bubble baths, she was starting to grow gills—and enough was enough. She was bored. Bored out of her mind.

It's not like she needed to spend every minute of every day with Harper. Miranda was a best friend, not some parasite who needed a constant infusion of Harper's energy to thrive. They needed *each other*, equally—or so Miranda had thought. Apparently, she'd thought wrong. Because here she was, alone. *Again.* On yet another Saturday night, playing Internet solitaire while Harper lived it up with the love of her life. So much for late-night rendezvous at the bar of choice, or Sunday brunches where they dissected every moment of the lame night before. No more of the late-night distress calls Miranda had complained about so much—never admitting, even to herself, how good it felt to be needed.

Not that Miranda begrudged her best friend her happiness—not much, at least.

"You wouldn't believe it, Rand," Harper told her. Constantly. "It's better than I ever could have imagined. Having him there for me? Always? It's amazing. It's so perfect. You'll see."

Sure, Miranda would see for herself. Someday. Maybe. Until then, she was growing intimately familiar with the whole outside-looking-in thing, turning herself into an impeccable third wheel in under a week. She'd always been a quick study.

Harper refused to elaborate on how it had happened, how one day Beth and Adam were going strong, and the next, Harper was the one in his arms, Beth kicked to the curb.

Not that vapid blondes like Beth ever stayed single for long—thirty seconds later, there she was, Kane Geary's latest conquest, floating along by his side as if she'd been there all along.

No, it was girls like Miranda who stayed single—for what seemed like forever. In all the years she'd longed for Kane, had he given her a second look? Had he ever once considered that her wit and charm might be worth ten of his bimbos, despite her stringy hair and lumpy physique?

No—guys like Kane, they never did. Probably, never would.

Her computer *dinged* with the sound of a new e-mail, and she opened it warily, expecting spam. More offers to increase her girth or introduce her to some "Hot XXX Girls NUDE NUDE NUDE." Who else would be sitting in front of their computer on a Saturday night but the people trying to sell that shit—and the people who actually bought it?

LOOKING FOR LOVE IN ALL THE WRONG PLACES? read the banner headline.

Great. Even cyberspace knew how pathetic she was.

```
Join MatchMadeInHaven.com, Grace's
first teen Internet dating site!
Find your true love with the click
of a mouse! After all—you've been
lonely too long. . . .
```

You can say that again, Miranda thought bitterly. And, for just a moment, she considered it. No one would ever have to know, she reasoned, and maybe, just maybe, this was her ticket to coupledom. Maybe there was someone out there, just like her, waiting for the right girl to come along. Could she really complain about being alone if she hadn't done everything in her power, *everything*, to fix the problem?

And then she caught herself, realizing the depths to which she was about to sink.

What are you thinking? she asked herself sternly, shaking her head in disgust. *You're not that desperate.*

At least, not yet.

They ate in silence.

The dining room table was large and long, too big for just the two of them. Kaia sat at one end, her father at the other, and for most of the meal, the quiet was punctuated only by the distant chattering of the maids in the kitchen and the occasional clatter of a silver Tiffany fork against the edge of Kaia's Rafaelesco plate. She saw her father wince at each *clang* and *scrape*—it didn't inspire her to be more careful.

Kaia would rather have been in the cavernous living room, eating take-out in front of the flat-screen, liquid-crystal TV, as usual. When you got down to it, she would have preferred to be back home in New York, eating in a chic TriBeCa bistro. Even holing up in her New York bedroom with a three-day-old bag of Doritos would have been preferable to having even one more meal in Grace, CA. Good food didn't change the fact that she was in exile, a prisoner, beholden to her parents' stupid whims. She didn't want to be stuck in the desert, stuck in his pretentious, *Architectural Digest* wannabe house, and she certainly didn't want to be stuck at the hand-crafted mahogany dining room table facing the man who was keeping her there. And despite her perpetual inability to read him, she was pretty sure he didn't want to be there, either. Yet there they sat, one night a month.

And the night stretched on, interminable.

"So, how's school?" her father finally asked.

"I wouldn't know," she answered lightly.

"Kaia . . ."

The warning note in his voice was subtle, but clear. *He talks to me like I'm one of his employees,* she thought, not for the first time.

"School's fine. Delightful," she offered. "I go every day. It's a truly wonderful experience. I'm simply learning ever so much. Is that what you want to hear?"

He sighed and shook his head. "I just want to hear the truth, Kaia. And I want to hear that you're happy."

"Sorry to disappoint, *Father*, but those are two different things—and, at the moment, they're mutually exclusive. You and Mother have seen to that."

His lips tightened, and Kaia braced for an angry response, some of that famous Keith Sellers temper, quick as lightning and just as deadly, but he kept it together. Barely. "This year isn't supposed to be a punishment, Kaia."

"Then why does it feel like one?"

"It's supposed to be a break," he continued, as if she hadn't spoken. "To give you and your mother some space. To give you some time to think about what you want your life to be."

"I want my life to be back to normal," Kaia spit out, immediately regretting it. She'd vowed not to let her guard down. Bad enough that she'd almost cried on the day he'd cut up all her credit cards—and *had* cried on the day her mother had shipped her off to the airport. She'd refused to give them the satisfaction of knowing she cared.

"Oh, Kaia. I wish I could help," he said, almost sounding like he meant it. "Maybe if I spent some more time at home. . . ."

"You really want to help?" Kaia asked, allowing a note of near sincerity to creep into her voice. She'd been waiting for the right moment for this, and there was no time like the present—right? "How about a temporary reprieve," she suggested. "Winter break's coming up, and I thought, maybe, just for a couple weeks—"

"You are *not* going back to the East Coast," he cut her off. "Not for two weeks, not for two days—you know the terms of our agreement."

"Agreement, right," she muttered. "Like I had a choice."

"What was that?" he snapped.

"I said, if this isn't a punishment, why do I feel like I'm in prison?" she asked, loud and clear.

"Katherine, that's quite enough whining for tonight." His measured tone masked an undercurrent of tightly bottled rage. The famous Keith Sellers temper was famous for a reason.

"It's *Kaia*," she reminded him.

"I named you *Katherine*," he countered, rising from the table. "I *let* you call yourself by that ridiculous name, but you'll always be Katherine, just like I'll always be your father, whether you like it or not."

"Trust me, I know," Kaia snarled. "If I could change that, along with the name, I would have done it a long time ago."

By the time he roared at her to go to her room, she was already out of her seat and halfway up the stairs.

Just another warm and fuzzy family dinner at the Sellers house.

Bon appétit.

It was almost midnight before Kaia's father had gone to sleep and she was able to sneak out of the house. She was still fuming about the way her parents felt they could run her life. They were mistaken. They could ship her across the country and strand her in the desert, but they couldn't stop her from slipping out of the mansion, driving twenty minutes down the deserted highway, pulling to a stop in front of a squat, nondescript, gray house, and scurrying up the walkway, head down to shield her face from prying eyes. They couldn't stop her from throwing open the door and falling into her lover's arms.

Her *lover*—she liked the sound of that. She'd had her share of guys, but never one she'd call a *lover*. The term was too adult, too mature for the puny prep school boys she'd toyed with back east—it was reserved for a man. And now she'd found one.

"Je m'oublie quand je suis avec toi," she murmured into his neck.

I forget myself when I'm with you.

He hated when she spoke French to him; it was too much of a reminder of his day job, and of their roles in the real world, beyond the walls of his cramped apartment, where he was a French teacher, she a student. He didn't want to remember—and she never wanted to forget.

The delicious scandal, the secrecy—why else was she there? It didn't hurt that he was sophisticated, worldly, movie-star handsome, that at least when they were alone in bed together, he treated her like a goddess—but really, the thrill of the forbidden had always been, and remained, the biggest draw. He was too shallow, too vain to be anything other than an object of illicit desire. She had no fairy-tale illusions of love—and knew he felt the same.

It's why they worked so well together.

"What are you thinking?" he asked idly, though she knew he didn't really care.

"I'm thinking you're a superficial, conceited, despicable human being, taking advantage of a sweet young girl like me." To Jack Powell, she could always speak some form of the truth—because the things they said to each other would never matter. Neither of them was in this for good conversation.

"And you're a callous, duplicitous, licentious girl who's out only for herself," he retorted in his clipped British accent, and kissed her roughly. "I can't get enough of you."

It was a match made in heaven—or somewhere a bit farther south.

chapter

2

"This . . . isn't . . . *so* . . . bad . . . ," Harper lied, panting for breath with every word.

Miranda slammed the big red button on her treadmill and nearly toppled to the ground as the moving track stopped short beneath her feet.

"Are you kidding?" she asked, glaring at Harper. "This has got to be the worst idea you've ever had."

Harper pushed her sweaty bangs out of her face and grimaced—she would never have suggested scamming Grace's only gym into giving them a free trial workout if she'd known it would be so much *work*. After all, working, on the first day of winter vacation? It went against everything she believed in.

But it would be worth it, she reminded herself, and began pedaling the stationary bike even faster. Harper usually steered clear of physical activity (unless you counted the kind that took place behind closed bedroom doors). But she'd always told herself that an aversion to exercise was a choice, not a necessity—if the time ever came that she needed to be in shape, she'd been sure it would be a snap.

The time had come. But the only thing snapping would be her bones, if she managed to fall off the exercise bike one more time.

"Maybe it's time to throw in the towel," Miranda suggested. She made a face and gestured toward the soggy towel she'd been using to wipe away her sweat. "Literally."

"No way." Harper smiled through gritted teeth. "We're just getting into the groove." She looked hatefully at the lithe bodies effortlessly working the machines all around her. Losers, all of them, judging by their baggy T-shirts, saggy shorts, and mis-sized sports bras—and yet none of them were gasping and panting like a wounded animal. Like Harper.

"So what's with the new work ethic?" Miranda asked, turning the treadmill back on and, with a sigh, continuing her plodding jog to nowhere.

"Hello—school ski trip coming up? Need to get in shape? Remember? Are you burning off calories or brain cells?"

"Funny." Miranda didn't show a hint of a smile. "But I don't buy it. You've got us up at the buttcrack of dawn, breaking a sweat. Just to get in shape so you can *ski*? And you don't even know how to ski."

Thanks for rubbing it in.

Harper knew it was ridiculous to want to impress Adam up on the slopes—and though she hated to admit it, she knew a couple hours on a stationary bike and a *Skiing for Dummies* book wouldn't help her keep up with someone who'd been on the slopes since he was nine. But it couldn't hurt to try, right? Adam was such the all-American athlete—skiing, swimming, running, he did it all with an ease that made Harper crazy. And his previous girl-friends had been the same way—even Beth, who'd never played on a team in her life, had a natural athletic grace that made Harper sick to watch.

She just wanted to make sure she measured up. Especially this weekend. This weekend, everything had to be perfect.

"Is this all to impress Adam?" Miranda persisted. Harper winced, hating the way her best friend could read every expression that flickered across her face. "Because you've known each other half your lives. Don't you think it's probably a little late to impress him? At least, more than you already have?"

Two months of dating—two months of fearing, every moment, that Adam would find out what she'd done to get him, would find out she wasn't the person he was, she hoped, falling in love with. Harper needed to impress him, all right, every moment. Because if she wasn't perfect—if they weren't perfect together—Harper suspected there was an understudy waiting in the wings who'd be only too happy to replace her. Harper wasn't about to give Beth the chance; but she also wasn't about to admit any of her pathetic insecurities out loud. She had far too much pride to expose that part of herself—even to Miranda.

"I just want this weekend to be good, all right?" she snapped, staring resolutely at the tiny TV screen hanging on the opposite wall, and pretending to care how Jerry Springer's latest guest had managed to accidentally sleep with her transsexual cousin.

"What makes this weekend any different from . . . oh!" A triumphant grin blossomed across Miranda's face. She hopped off the machine and grabbed a handlebar on Harper's bike, forcing Harper to face her. "Are you telling me that this weekend is . . . ?"

Harper felt a tingling heat spread across her cheeks and jerked her head away. She couldn't be blushing. She never blushed.

"This is it, isn't it?" Miranda pressed on eagerly. "WFS. Are you kidding me? After all this time, you haven't . . ."

WFS.

Weekend For Sex. Harper and Miranda had coined the term a couple years ago, the first time Harper's parents had left her alone for the weekend. Justin Diamond, the JV lacrosse captain and her first serious boyfriend, had pulled into the driveway five minutes after her parents had left. (And about five minutes later, he'd been ready to pull out again.)

Harper gave Miranda a curt nod.

"WFS!" Miranda repeated in a hushed and wondrous tone. "I don't believe it."

"Rand, can we drop it?" Harper asked irritably, pedaling harder. Miranda was making it sound like she just hopped into bed with anything that moved—as if she had no patience, no discrimination, no self-restraint.

And, okay, it had been a long time since she'd made a guy wait so long. She knew that Beth was still a virgin, knew that sleeping with Adam would probably be the fastest and surest way to win his affection—but she wanted more than that. Adam was worth more than some guy, more than all of them put together.

Feeling like she was about to pass out, Harper sighed and stopped pedaling.

"Oh, thank God," Miranda breathed, staggering off the treadmill and taking a long gulp from her water bottle. She tossed it over to Harper. "Here—you look even worse than I feel." .

Harper bristled at the suggestion (okay, observation of the obvious) that she was a tiny bit out of shape, but gulped down half the bottle before passing it back. "I didn't *have* to stop," she boasted. "I've just got a lot of errands to run before I go to work."

Work. The word still sounded strange coming out of her mouth.

"Work?" Miranda repeated incredulously. "Work on what? Your nails?"

Harper looked away—she'd held off on telling Miranda about her little problem, but this moment would have had to come, sooner or later. "I got a job," she mumbled, staring over her shoulder as Jerry's guest tried to strangle her cousin with the microphone cord.

"A what?"

"A job," Harper spit out, finally facing her. "I got a job, okay? My stupid parents wouldn't pay for the ski trip, and I needed to go, so I just—oh, forget it."

It was so humiliating. She was, after all, Harper Grace—as in, Grace, California. The town had been named for her family's mining company, and for decades they had ruled like desert royalty. And then, years before Harper had been born—no more copper. No more mines. And just like that—no more money.

At least, if you believed her parents' endless whining.

But they had enough to get by. Enough for "important" things—they just didn't understand the meaning of the word. And so Harper had to carry on the Grace name, the Grace legacy, all on her own. And if that meant a few weeks of menial labor—she shivered at the thought—so be it.

Miranda frowned, knowing better than to make light of Harper's situation—not when it involved cash flow, and definitely not when it involved working hard, working for other people, working in *public*.

"Why didn't you tell me?" she asked, quietly. "Maybe I could have—"

"Don't even say it," Harper snapped. Graces didn't accept handouts. Not from anyone.

"So, where are you working?" Miranda finally asked, after a long and awkward pause.

"It doesn't matter." Like she was going to tell Miranda about her humiliating saga, traipsing from one bar to the next, only to be turned away for being too young. Not too young to drink—or too young to flirt with—but that was as far as any of these loser bartenders had been willing to go. She'd tried the Lost and Found, the Cactus Cantina, and then in desperation even Bourquin's Coffee Shop and the decrepit vintage cloth-ing store, Classic Rags—but in the end, only one place had had any openings. And no wonder—it was the last place any sane person would have chosen to work. Which meant plenty of openings for those poor saps with no choice at all.

She made a show of checking her watch and frowned as if she had somewhere far more important to be.

"I have to get out of here, Rand," she lied, hurrying

toward the locker room as fast as her weary, leaden legs could carry her.

"Is this weekend really worth that much to you?" Miranda called, scurrying to catch up.

Harper just shot her a look—the WFS look—and Miranda nodded. That said it all.

On her walk home, Miranda couldn't stop thinking about Harper—maybe that's why she didn't see him. Her brain was stuck on the fact that her best friend, who usually told her everything—usually more than she wanted to know—had started keeping secrets. There was the job thing. The WFS—did that count as a secret too? Harper had clearly gone out of her way never to mention it—but then, she'd kept unnaturally quiet on almost everything having to do with her relationship with Adam. Oh, she talked about Adam plenty. Adam was, these days, almost all she talked about. How wonderful he was. How happy he made her. How much he loved being with her. And on, and on, until it seemed like their friendship had turned into nothing more than an Adam Morgan love-fest. But they never talked about anything real, like how Harper felt about being in her first serious relationship. Or how Miranda felt like her best friend was slipping away from her. And they never, ever talked about the biggest secret of all: how Harper and Adam had gotten together in the first place.

What had happened that day, when Adam went off to a swim meet, Beth stayed in town, and Harper inexplicably showed up the next morning with Adam hanging on her arm?

To be fair, Miranda had never come right out and asked Harper what had happened—that same night, they'd had a massive fight, and Harper had left Miranda crying and alone in the middle of the woods. Left her there for no good reason—and come home with everything she'd ever wanted, while Miranda had, as always, come home alone.

Harper had never really apologized. Miranda suspected, in fact, that in the warm glow of Adam-inspired happiness, Harper had totally forgotten. Miranda forgave her anyway. Like always. But that didn't mean things had gone back to normal. Miranda and Harper had always been a twosome—but now, Harper plus Adam made two. And two plus Miranda made a crowd. There was this new part of Harper's life that Miranda couldn't have access to, couldn't really understand. She was too embarrassed to even mention any of this to Harper, didn't want to be seen as a lonely and pathetic third wheel, someone to be included out of pity. Out of obligation.

So there was another secret.

How many secrets would it take, Miranda wondered, to kill a friendship?

The question kept bouncing around in her head—it was all she could focus on. And that's why she didn't see him—not until he was, literally, on top of her.

"Can you watch where you're going?"

The boy who'd slammed past Miranda turned back at the sound of her angry snarl. He froze in the middle of the sidewalk when he realized whom he'd hit.

"I'm . . . I'm sorry," Miranda stammered, backing away. "I didn't—"

"No, *I'm sorry*," he interrupted, with exaggerated

21

solemnity. "I didn't realize that I'd bumped into the high and mighty Miranda. What a fool I am."

"Greg . . . ," she began, then stopped herself. What could she say? *Sorry I went on a few dates with you and blew you off? Sorry that, even though you're smart and funny and liked me a lot, it just wasn't going to work?* Or how about, *Sorry that you overheard me telling my best friend that I deserve better than you?* Miranda didn't think there was a Miss Manners–prescribed etiquette for the situation, but none of the most obvious options seemed particularly appropriate.

"Sorry I yelled, Greg," she finally continued. "I didn't realize it was you."

"Oh, she remembers my name," he crowed, not meeting her eyes. "I'm so honored."

"Greg, can we just—do you have to . . ."

"Do I have to what?" he asked loudly, drawing curious stares from two women pushing their strollers across the street. "Do I have to stand here and pretend I care what you have to say?" He paused, and pretended to think it over. "Now that you mention it—no, I don't."

He brushed past her and strode down the street, pausing a few feet away to shout something back to her.

"I do sincerely apologize for bumping into you—you *deserve much better* than that."

If nothing else, the encounter—her first run-in with Greg since the "unfortunate incident"—should have proved to Miranda that her instincts had been right: She was too good for that immature jerk. But telling herself that didn't help much. She'd been feeling guilty for weeks about the things she'd said about Greg—and the look on his face when he'd overheard.

She had hoped that maybe, since all this time had passed, he'd have cooled down, be willing to forgive her, assure her that she wasn't such a cold and horrible person. That maybe they could even be friends.

Apparently not.

Harper had lied—not a first. She had hours to go before she officially entered the miserable ranks of the employed. But she'd needed to escape before Miranda pried more information out of her about her job, or her boyfriend. It was exhausting, trying so hard to keep her best friend out of the loop. Sometimes, it was easier to just be alone.

So here she was, hours to kill on Grace's main drag. As a general rule, the town offered only two leisure options: shopping and boozing. And since she didn't plan to show up plastered for her first day of work, those options narrowed to one.

Time to pre-spend that first paycheck. (The second one would go to her parents, to pay back the money they'd loaned her—but as far as she was concerned, the first money she'd ever earned for herself was already earmarked for a fabulous new ensemble that would make her shine up on the slopes as much as she shined on the ground.)

First stop had been the local video store. She'd snuck in, skulked around the sparse fitness section for a few minutes, and then grabbed the cheapest and most painless-looking workout videos she could find: *Sweatin' to the Oldies, Pilates for Beginners*, and a Paula Abdul dance aerobics tape clearly left over from 1987. After throwing a wad of cash at the clerk, she stuffed the tapes into the bottom of her gym bag and raced out of the store, hoping no one had spotted her. She wasn't about to break a sweat in public again, not after her pathetic showing this morning, but she also wasn't about to let anyone know she'd be sweating to the oldies at home with Richard Simmons. The potential humiliation factor was through the roof.

Next stop: Angie's, Grace's only "fine clothing shop." Harper usually shopped online—most Grace gear was pretty much a fashion faux pas waiting to happen—but the ski trip was fast approaching, and she had no time to waste waiting for a package that, given the incompetence of her local postal workers, might never arrive. Just one problem: Angie's was a desert clothing store, and even in the middle of winter, their cold-weather selection was limited to a shelf of thick socks, thin gloves, and a few wool sweaters covered with giant snowflakes.

"Pathetic, isn't it?"

Harper recognized the voice and turned around slowly to meet the familiar smirk.

"Fancy meeting you here," she greeted him with a smile.

"A true delight," Kane drawled sarcastically, pulling out a pack of cigarettes and lighting up—despite the prominently placed NO SMOKING sign just above his head.

If Harper was surprised to spot him in a women's clothing store, she didn't let on, nor did she reveal her true delight at running into him. They had so few chances to speak privately these days—and of course it was only in private that they could crow about the triumph of their secret plan. Harper never got tired of winning, and she never got tired of rehashing her victories. Too bad Kane and Kaia were the only ones who could ever know about this, the greatest victory of all.

"See anything you like?" Kane asked.

Harper dropped the light blue cashmere scarf she'd been fingering—it was the only worthwhile item in the store. And it was gorgeous. It also cost about as much as the entire ski trip—and thus was way out of her league. Not that she'd ever admit it to Kane.

"Nada. This place is a fashion wasteland," she complained, grabbing a cigarette from him after deciding that the clerk was too immersed in her latest trashy romance novel to notice. "So, having a good time?"

He raised an eyebrow. "Shopping? Surely you jest."

She smacked him lightly on the arm. "Not the store, Kane—the girl. You. Beth. Is it everything you'd hoped for?"

His face finally broke into a wide grin.

"And more," he confided. "She can't get enough of me. And no wonder. You should have seen the look on her face when Adam showed up raging about what she'd done. She had no idea what the hell he was talking about. Totally crushed." He waggled his eyebrows at Harper and smirked, as he did every time he fondly recounted this point in the story. "I, of course, was there to pick up the pieces. You can imagine she'd be quite grateful."

"That's nothing," Harper claimed. "You should have seen the look on Adam's face when he saw the pictures. He . . ." But she trailed off, for there was nothing particularly amusing about the memory of her oldest friend's reaction to seeing the doctored photos of Beth and Kane. He'd collapsed in on himself, and Harper had been the cause. Knowing she could alleviate his pain with a few words— confess that the pictures were fake, that she and Kane were to blame, that Beth was, as always, pure and innocent—that had been the hardest part of the whole thing. But she couldn't do it—wouldn't do it. She wasn't proud of what she'd done, but there had been no other way.

"Come on, Grace, don't get sentimental on me now," Kane charged. "This is a time for swagger and celebration."

"Sometimes I just wonder . . ."

"What, whether we did the right thing?"

"Well, don't you?" she countered.

"Why bother?" he asked, smirking. "What's done is done. Adam and Beth were doomed—we just helped things along a bit. Think of it as a mercy killing."

"I suppose Adam is much better off now without all that dead weight," Harper mused.

"Hey, watch it," Kane cautioned her in mock anger. "That's my girlfriend you're talking about."

"Your *girlfriend*, right." Harper took a long drag on her cigarette, relishing the sharp taste of the smoke billowing out of her mouth. Adam hated it when she smoked, so she'd been trying to cut back. It had seemed a small price to pay, but God, she missed that nicotine buzz. "I guess I should congratulate you, now that we're coming up on two months. What is this, your longest relationship ever?"

"Very funny, Grace." But the smile had disappeared from his face. "Did you ever stop to think this one might be different?"

"Did I ever stop to think that the great Kane Geary, who's made a life's work of dating his way through town, who gets bored after about ten minutes of *anything*, might actually be tamed by Beth, of all people? Blond, bland, boring, *Beth*?" She finished off the cigarette and pondered the question. "No, I guess the thought never occurred to me."

"You underestimate her, Grace. You always have."

"And you *over*estimate her, Kane," she pointed out. "That's the part of this I've never understood. Why Beth, of all people? She thought you were scum, she was dating Adam, she's *so* not your type. Why her?"

Kane smiled cryptically.

"Why not?"

The most memorable moment in my life was the time when I . . .

Growing up in a small town, I always believed that someday I would . . .

If there's one thing I know in life, it's that I . . .

Pathetic!

Beth slumped against the wall of the kitchen, ignoring the sticky grease patches that quickly dampened her polyester uniform. Her college applications were due in a couple weeks, and if she wanted to make up for her horrible SAT scores . . . She shivered at the memory of filling in all those tiny bubbles as tears spattered against the test booklet. It was bad enough Adam had broken up with her without any warning, had accused her of cheating on him, had tossed her away without a second thought—but she could never forgive him for doing it all the night before the SATs. If he were trying to ruin her life, he'd made a pretty damn good start.

No, if she didn't come up with an amazing application essay, something that would blow the mind of any admissions officer who read it, she could kiss her future goodbye.

"Manning! Table seven's still waiting for their food!"

her manager called. One of the other waitresses, blowing past on her way back to the main dining area, shot her a dirty look: *You may think you're better than us,* it said. *You're wrong.*

Without college, she'd have a future, all right—a long and unprosperous life of flipping burgers at the Nifty Fifties diner, smiling pathetically at all her former classmates as they breezed through on spring break before heading back to their real lives in the real world. Not like she had any time to deal with her applications, the magic ticket to a new life—she was working double shifts to pay for this ski trip that Kane was insisting on, and every spare minute was spent at home, babysitting her little brothers. *Leave it to me to get busier over winter break,* she thought bitterly.

Beth stood up and tried to muster enough energy to face her customers, still furiously writing and rewriting in her head.

I'm a boring girl from a boring town, but I make a mean burger and fries. . . .

"Waitress! We've been waiting for our food *forever!*"

Beth looked over to table seven—and almost turned on her heel and fled back to the kitchen. Spending her vacation at the diner, mopping up spilled milk shakes, ducking grease spatter, and taking orders from every surly, hygienically challenged customer who walked through the door, was bad enough. This was worse. It was what she hated most about this job: taking orders from her friends.

Scratch that—her *former* friends.

Christie, Nikki, Marcy, and Darcy were all dating guys from the basketball team. Which guys? Beth could never keep track—sometimes, she wondered if they could, either.

Before she'd started dating Adam, back when she was just another faceless nobody, they'd refused to acknowledge her existence. Oh, they knew her name, all right—the Haven High seniors had been trapped in one building or another together since kindergarten. There were no strangers in a small town. But you would never have known it, not from the blank stares when she crossed their path, from the way they looked right through her, as if she didn't exist. As if she were nothing.

Then she'd started dating Adam—captain of the basketball team (and every other team that mattered), perennial homecoming king, Haven High's golden boy—and suddenly, the Nikkis and the Christies of the world had welcomed her with open arms. More than that, they'd *begged* her to join them.

Come to Christie's sleepover party and home spa day!
Hang with us at Nikki's for tanning and iced Frappaccinos!
Let's all buy this super-cute pink scarf—and then wear them on the same day!

And so, despite her overstuffed schedule, despite never trusting them or her newfound status, she'd given in. Any free time she'd had that didn't go to the newspaper or to the diner or to her family or to Adam—and granted, after all that, there wasn't much left—went to the girls. It had been fun; it had also been, as she now realized, a mistake. A big one.

For as far as they knew, she'd cheated on Adam, broken his heart. So in their eyes, he was still Prince Charming, while she'd been transformed into the wicked witch.

She'd been a stranger, she'd become a friend—now, apparently, she was the enemy.

"Waitress!" Nikki called, waving her over. "Is there a problem? We're starving."

You know my name, Beth retorted—silently. Aloud, she said only, "It'll be here as soon as possible, Nikki." Through gritted teeth.

"It better be," Nikki growled.

"Or what?" The words slipped out before Beth could stop herself.

"What did you say?" Nikki asked with incredulity. She turned to her left. "Christie, is it just me, or is the waitress being rather rude?"

"I'm sure she wouldn't be rude, Nikki," Christie responded in a voice oozing with false goodwill. "Since she knows that then we'd simply have no choice but to complain to the manager."

"You're right. I'm sure I must have misheard," Nikki conceded. "You can go now, waitress," she said haughtily, flicking Beth away like a speck of dirt on her white pants. "Just bring us the food when it's ready—and try not to *cheat* us on the bill. If you can help yourself."

Beth forced a smile and walked away with a steady step. Maybe, if she pretended hard enough that the mockery didn't bother her, it would stop. Or, at the very least, her feigned indifference might eventually transform itself into something real. But for now, it was all still an act—and the show wasn't over yet. She was only steps away when she heard Marcy's intentionally loud complaint: "I just don't know *what's* wrong with the service these days."

In spite of herself, Beth hesitated, and turned around.

"Well, you know what my mother always says," Nikki replied, glaring directly at Beth. "These days, it's impossible to find good help."

Beth wanted to crawl into a dark hole. She wanted to quit her job, run home, hide under the covers, and wait there until graduation. But instead, she just strode across the restaurant to take her next order, figuring that, at the very least, her shift couldn't get any worse.

Wrong again.

"Hi, beautiful."

Kane peeked his head out from behind a menu and smiled up at her. Surprise.

Beth nibbled on the inside of her lip and hoped he wouldn't notice the tears that had formed at the edges of her eyes. She hated for him to see her like this—in uniform, serving people, being humiliated. Had he seen her with Nikki and crew? Had he heard?

"What are you doing here?" she asked, masking her distress with annoyance.

"I heard the place has the cutest waitresses in town," he deadpanned, grabbing her hand and twining her fingers through his own. "Thought I'd come check it out."

"So what's the verdict?" Beth asked, flushing.

"Jury's still out," he said, rising to give her a kiss. "But maybe you'd like to offer a bribe that would tip the scales?"

Beth wriggled out of his grasp.

"Kane, stop," she protested, backing away. She didn't want him near her. Not with grease patches dotting her shirt, not when she smelled like coleslaw and onion rings.

"I asked you not to come here when I'm working," she snapped. "It's distracting."

"Your wish is my command—I'm out of here," Kane promised, a knowing smile fixed on his face. "I just wanted to give you this."

He handed her a small box, elegantly wrapped in light silver paper. Beth didn't know what to say.

"It's not my birthday, and—"

"I just saw it and thought of you," he explained, resting a hand on her lower back. "Open it."

Slightly flushed, Beth carefully pulled off the wrapping paper and lifted the lid of the box. Inside lay a beautiful sky blue scarf. It was exactly the same shade as her eyes.

"Kane, it's beautiful!" she exclaimed. She lifted it to her cheek and sighed at the soft caress of the fabric.

"Is this—?"

"Cashmere," he confirmed.

"But it's too nice, I couldn't—"

"You'll look beautiful in it," he assured her, wrapping it softly around her neck. "And this way, you'll be nice and cozy up in the mountains this weekend." He raised an eyebrow. "Just in case *I'm* not enough to keep you warm."

Beth laughed and snuggled against him—suddenly, she didn't care what she was wearing, or how she looked or smelled. She just cared that she had a warm body to lean against, warm lips to kiss.

"Meet me back here at the end of my shift?" she whispered as they finally broke apart.

"You can count on me."

And she was beginning to wonder if it might just be true.

www.matchmadeinhaven.com
username: Spitfire
password: MStevens88
Friday's entrée at the Haven High cafeteria:
meat loaf

(Miranda thought this last log-in requirement was a master stroke—how else would the Web site screen out all the perverts and cyberfreaks?) She hit enter, and the final version of her profile popped up on the screen.

User Profile: Spitfire
Sex: female
Age: 17
Height: 5'2"

(Okay, so she'd added an extra inch and a half—but who knows, maybe she was still growing.)

Favorite color: scarlet
Favorite food: ———-
If I were an animal, I'd be: an elephant

(It wasn't sexy, but had the virtue of being true.)

Best lie I've ever told: Mom, you look great today—have you lost weight? And can I have a raise in my allowance?
Celebrity I most look like: Scarlett Johannson

(Um . . . maybe if you squinted? While you were high?)

Three things I can't live without: 1) my iPod, 2) my best friend, 3) chocolate chip cookies

I am . . . always ready to laugh, or to make you laugh. Honest, loyal, fun (and totally willing to hold a grudge on your behalf).

You are . . . someone who thinks these questions are as stupid as I do. Someone who knows how to have a good time without making an ass of himself—and if the latter can't be helped, at least is able to laugh at himself. Someone who knows what the word "latter" means. Basically, you're smart, funny, confident, and you love that I'm all those things too.

The confident thing was a lie, of course, but she'd thought it would look good, and might attract the right kind of guy. The kind who wasn't a desperate freak too pathetic to find his own flesh-and-blood dates. If any of the guys on matchmadeinhaven.com actually fit that profile—Miranda was seriously skeptical.

But, crazy or not, she'd decided to go for it. What, other than the final shreds of her dignity, did she have to lose?

chapter

3

"Here's your uniform, and here's your mop."

"My . . . mop?" Harper took the outstretched polyester hoop skirt, holding it between the tips of two fingers as if afraid of catching its germs. She just stared at the mop, however—no way was she touching that thing, much less pushing it around.

"What, did you think I was going to start you out as a waitress?" Mr. White, the Nifty Fifties manager, threw his head back and burst into mean-spirited laughter, his double chins jiggling in time with his throaty cackles. Finally he stopped, rubbing his bald spot thoughtfully. "Well, you're pretty enough to be out front, I'll give you that."

Harper held herself still as his beady eyes swept over her body. He was gross—but if it meant losing the mop, well . . . let him look.

"But you've got no experience," he continued. "You can start training as a waitress as soon as your supervisor thinks you're ready."

"My supervisor? Aren't you my supervisor?" Harper looked around the restaurant, wondering which of the crater-faced losers would be bossing her around. Maybe this was a good thing, she thought—at least she wouldn't have to humiliate herself, serving people she knew. Safe in back with the mop, she could work completely under-cover.

"Me?" Mr. White expelled another hearty chuckle. "I don't supervise people at *your* level. No, I've got someone perfect for the job. In fact, you probably know her." He stuck his bulbous head out of the kitchen door, bellowing, "Manning! Get back here for a minute."

Harper's knees almost gave out, and she was forced to lean against the grimy wall for support. *Of course,* she thought. She should have known.

"Yes, Mr. White?" Beth bounded into the kitchen and stopped short when she saw Harper, looking horrified. Harper couldn't even take her usual pleasure at the sight of Beth in her tacky uniform, knowing full well that soon, she'd be sharing the same fate.

"Good news, I'm giving you a little helper," the man-ager said shortly. "Harper Grace, meet Beth Manning, your new boss."

"Oh, we've met," Beth said coolly.

"Yep, I figured." He thrust the mop handle into Harper's hands and kicked a rolling bucket of soapy water toward her. She squealed and squirmed away as some of it sloshed over the top and splattered onto her faux Manolos.

"I want Harper here to start with the basics: floors, toilets, spills—you know the drill. And don't be giving her any special treatment just because you two are friends—got that?"

"Oh yes, Mr. White," Beth assured him, a broad smile crossing her face. "I know exactly what to do with her."

Harper leaned back against the wall again and clenched the mop tightly.

You can handle this, she told herself sternly.

She just hoped it was true.

Adam usually counted the days until the start of basketball season. Though too modest to admit it aloud, he knew exactly how good he was at nearly every sport Haven High had to offer. Last year he'd led the league in lacrosse assists, and as captain of the swim team he'd just set a new school record in the butterfly relay—but there was nothing like basketball. It wasn't just the adulation of the town during basketball season: the cheers of the crowd, the triumphant headlines, the adoring cheerleaders—though all of that helped. It was the game itself, the rough, heavy feel of the ball cradled in his hands, the flicker of weightlessness in those moments his feet left the ground, the cool certainty of a perfect shot, when the ball flew from your fingers, sailing through the air in a perfect arc. You could close your eyes, turn away—and just wait for the soft, satisfying *swish*.

He'd woken at dawn that morning and spent the day bouncing around the house, filled with nervous energy, just waiting for nightfall, for the first practice of the season. Now that he was finally stepping into the locker room, he suddenly realized he hadn't felt so happy, so relaxed in weeks. And then, in an instant, it all went to shit.

"What are you doing here?" he asked sourly.

"I—"

"Never mind, I don't want to hear it." Adam turned

away and flung open his locker, throwing his gym bag to the floor and pulling off his T-shirt in one fast, fluid motion. He wanted to get out of there as quickly as possible. He hadn't spoken to Kane since the night it had all gone down. And to run into him now—here, of all places, the site of his betrayal—

"I'm on the team," Kane said calmly. "Where else would I be?"

"You're not on the team," Adam growled. Kane had played ball for Haven High back in tenth grade. He'd lasted a month. Kane had been the best player they had, by far—but after he'd missed two practices in a row, Coach Hanford had thrown him off the squad. Now Adam was the best player they had. But only by default. "Coach Hanford would never let you back on the team."

"Hanford's out," Kane retorted. "Or didn't you get the memo? Retired to Arizona. And, lucky for me, Coach Wilson isn't such a hard ass—he seemed quite persuaded by what I had to say."

Adam pulled on his team shorts and slammed the locker shut.

"How did you—" he stopped himself. He couldn't speak to Kane, couldn't look at him, without the bile rising in his throat. Without remembering the pictures he'd seen, of Beth and Kane, in the locker room, after hours, in each other's arms.

"Could be fun, bro," Kane suggested. "Like old times, you and me—"

"I'm not your *bro,*" Adam spit out, finally facing him. "I don't know what you think you're doing here, and I don't care. Just stay the hell away from me."

He brushed past Kane and headed for the door—he suddenly needed to be out on the court, to slam a basketball into the backboard. Hard.

"Now, is that any way to talk to a friend?" Kane called out after him.

We're not friends. And I guess we never were.

But out loud, Adam said nothing. Kane had thrown away any right he'd had to call himself a friend. He'd trashed their friendship; he'd trashed Adam's life. And now Kane had the nerve to speak to him? *Here?* Had the nerve to rejoin *his* team? Was he trying to destroy yet another part of Adam's life? Adam's love for basketball was pure, and it was clean, and he wasn't going to let Kane infect it, or steal it away.

Not this time.

Not again.

Beth had always been a "nice girl." She thought of the phrase just like that, in quotes, because she was so used to hearing the words in someone else's voice. "Be a nice girl," insisted her mother. "Such a nice girl!" her teachers all glowed. Other people's voices, telling her who she was, what she should be. But all she ever heard in her own, silent voice these days was a warning.

Nice girls finish last.

And here was Harper, the perfect object lesson—the antithesis of nice, and she always walked away with everything. She was beautiful, she was popular, she was *mean*—and yet still, she'd taken home the prize. Beth's boyfriend. (*Ex*-boyfriend, she reminded herself.) And now here she was, at Beth's mercy.

Beth could do the right thing, the *nice* thing—show her all the shortcuts, the places White would never check her work, ways to take an extra-long break; Beth could get her bumped up to the waitstaff in a few days.

Or . . . she could take a cue from Harper and throw nice out the window. She could be strict. Cruel. *Mean.*

And as it turned out, she was a natural.

"Well, what are you waiting for?" Beth asked caustically, as Harper stood frozen with the mop. "A written invitation? The bathroom's that way—get to work."

Harper trudged off down the corridor. Realizing that she'd neglected to change into her uniform, Beth was about to call out after her—then decided against it. Let Harper figure out on her own why she might not want to scrub a toilet in her street clothes. Instead, she followed Harper silently down the hall. After all, she was a supervisor now. It was time to get to work.

"Are you just going to stand there all day and watch me?" Harper asked, after she'd been sweeping the mop back and forth for fifteen minutes.

"If that's what it takes," Beth answered snidely. "You're doing it all wrong—might as well just start over again."

"What?" Harper cried. "No way."

"Well, if you want me to call Mr. White and see what he thinks . . ."

Harper sighed and shrugged her shoulders. "Fine—you're the boss."

Beth was amused by how much the words thrilled her. Everywhere else in this town, Harper was in charge. Suddenly, Beth was the one with all the power. And she loved it already.

"I don't know how Adam put up with you for all that time," Harper mumbled under her breath.

"What was that?" Beth asked sharply.

"Oh, nothing," Harper replied in a poisonously sweet voice. "Just wondering to myself what I should wear on my date tonight. My *boyfriend* is taking me somewhere special. It's our two-month anniversary, you know."

Beth knew. And she knew what had happened two months ago. In one day, Adam had both hooked up with Harper and decided Beth was cheating on him. Beth had long wondered which had come first. But she wasn't about to ask.

She walked out of the bathroom without a word and back down to the kitchen, where she grabbed a fresh packet of sponges. Then she rejoined Harper and tossed her one.

"You'll want to get down on your knees and really scrub those hard-to-clean stains," she explained, pointing to a random spot at her feet. "There's one now."

Harper looked at the sponge with disdain. "My hands and knees? On *this* floor? You have got to be kidding me."

"Hey, if you can't cut it, you're welcome to quit," Beth suggested, impressed by her own icy tone. Where was all this coming from? Was this who, deep down, she really was? Whatever the answer, if felt too good to stop. "Until then," she continued, smiling as Harper slowly got down on all fours, "like you said—I'm the boss."

Kane didn't like surprises—or mysteries. So it was bad enough when Adam, totally unexpectedly, had refused to forgive him for the Beth thing even after all this time.

Worse was the fact that Kane couldn't figure out why.

Yes, he'd stolen Adam's girlfriend. Obviously, he wasn't expecting a thank-you. But this? The silent treatment for two months, as if they were both ten years old again and Kane had smashed up Adam's brand-new bike? (And even back then, it had only taken Adam a week to forgive and forget.)

She was, after all, just a girl. And Kane had seen her first.

The Beth Manning they'd grown up with had been nothing; a plain, faded face in the crowd, about as exciting as an old T-shirt at the bottom of your drawer. Familiar, reliable, and not so ugly that you'd *never* wear it—but best saved until you were desperate.

Kane had known who she was, of course—he knew all the girls. But knowing and caring are two different things—and in this case, they'd been a universe apart.

Then came sophomore year. The first day of school. And into their bio lab had walked a goddess: slim, tall, with perfect skin, a willowy figure, and glossy golden hair. It was Beth 2.0, new and improved, and from the moment she'd flowed through the door, Kane had vowed to have her.

He'd just never expected it would take so much effort.

A girl like that, a wallflower, a nobody, should have been falling all over herself in gratitude for attention from someone like him. Guys like Kane didn't speak to girls like Beth Manning—or at least, they hadn't before the Change. But there was no gratitude, and she seemed immune to his considerable charm.

So he'd enlisted Adam's help—his *best friend*, he'd thought, remembering with derision. Adam was her lab partner, and his job was simple: Pave the way, reel her in, let her see that the A-list crowd wasn't so bad, that she could trust guys like Adam. And, by extension, Adam's good buddy Kane—that she could let her guard down. It was a gambit they'd used a lot in those days, letting Adam's basic decency lure the girls in, under the assumption that Kane, too, must be a "nice guy." Even if it wasn't readily apparent. It took them a bit longer to figure out the truth—and by then, Kane had generally gotten what he needed out of them. It worked both ways: Sometimes Kane played the wingman, dazzling the ladies with his charm and then passing them along to Adam. Good old solid, reliable, dull Adam. It was a good game, and they'd worked well together, partners in crime, wading through the shallow waters of Haven hotties.

And together, they'd worked out rule #1: Any girl was fair game—as long as you saw her first.

So perhaps Kane could be forgiven for trusting his partner, for assuming that the rules of the game still applied and that Adam would work his magic and send Beth flying into his arms. Imagine his surprise, then, to find that Adam had decided to keep this one for himself.

It was a betrayal, and it had led to a loss—a public one. And that, Kane could not forget. He'd kept quiet, played along—it wouldn't do to make a fuss, to be driven to unseemly emotion, not over a *girl*—but he'd also known that it wasn't over. No girl could be allowed to choose someone over him. Not even Adam.

It had taken more than a year, but he'd gotten his way.

Beth, who had only grown more beautiful since that first sighting, had seen the light. She'd rectified her mistake, and this time, she'd made the right choice. And if ever Kane got a little bored with the whole relationship thing, he just reminded himself of his struggle. This was his rightful reward, and he was going to enjoy it. If Adam was man enough to have a relationship, to make this girl fall in love with him, then so was Kane.

And he certainly didn't need Adam's approval. Or his forgiveness. Kane didn't need anyone. But if their friendship was going to end, *Kane* would be the one to make the decision—and Kane wasn't ready for that yet. Without Adam, Grace was almost too boring to bear. So he'd talked his way back onto the team, bearing the humiliation of having to beg the new coach for a shot. If he stayed in Adam's face, reminded him of how well they'd worked together, as a team, eventually Adam would have to give up the childish grudge. In the meantime, Kane would do the diligent teammate thing: go to the practices, run the windsprints, pretend he cared. Kane would do whatever he needed to do, he resolved, except one thing: apologize.

Eventually, Beth got bored and left Harper alone with the mop and bucket.

It's like they always say, thought Harper, *ignore a bully and she'll go away.* She'd just never been on the wrong side of that equation before.

This job was, if possible, even worse than Harper had imagined. But if she kept her eye on the prize, on Adam, then maybe the time would just slip by—she'd be in his arms again soon enough.

His arms—that was good. She pictured them wrapped around her, warm and strong. In her mind's eye, they curled up together on a soft couch, next to a giant picture window. A beautiful mountain range loomed in the distance, and snow pelted the windows, but Harper was so warm, so cozy in Adam's arms. She could, if she closed her eyes, almost feel his presence . . .

"Harper, is that you?"

Harper's eyes flew open to see those joined-at-the-hip dolts Marcy and Darcy, staring at her in horror.

"Harper, what are you doing . . . here?"

She dropped the mop in alarm and backed away, struggling to recover the blasé veneer she would need to make it through this. "I'm just, I—"

"Harper works here now," Beth said cheerfully, suddenly appearing behind the wonder twins. "I'm sorry, I must have forgotten to put up the sign saying the restroom was closed for cleaning. Oops!"

She smiled at Harper, who knew it had been no accident. Just as Beth's sudden arrival had been no coincidence. She'd come to witness Harper's humiliation; she'd come to gloat.

"Is something wrong, Harper?" she asked sweetly. "Because otherwise, you really should get back to work."

Harper drew in a sharp breath and held it for several moments.

"I'm all done in here," she finally said. "Later, ladies." She gave them a jaunty grin and walked away, towing the bucket behind her.

It had been a humiliating encounter, but there would be no long-term fallout, she assured herself. Nobody who counted listened to anything those airheads had to say. Still, when she tried to send herself back to that comforting vision of her and Adam cuddling in the ski lodge, she was just too angry—Beth's smug face kept breaking into her reverie, hovering over her like the Cheshire Cat.

So Harper did what any good, disgruntled employee would do: She went with it. She imagined Beth coming in to check on her, ordering her around—and then she imagined herself picking up the giant bucket of hot, scummy water and dumping it over Beth's smug little head.

She kept that image fixed in her mind, varying it for fun: Beth covered in ketchup and mustard, Beth smothered in relish, Beth drowning in a vat of cole slaw and pickle juice.

The possibilities were nearly endless, and Harper mentally ran through them all. The rest of her shift raced by in a flash. Time flies when you're having fun.

Kaia's father's brand-new, mint-condition BMW had a 5-liter capacity, 10 cylinders, a 500 horsepower output, a V-10 engine, and 383 pounds per foot maximum torque.

It also, she discovered once she got out on the empty highway, had a dead battery. Or an overheated exhaust system. Or maybe it was a torn carburetor belt.

Who knew? And, really, who cared? All that mattered was that the car wouldn't go anywhere, and she was stranded. In the middle of nowhere.

Typical, she thought, slumping down against the smooth black leather of the front seat and waiting for the tow truck she'd called. There was nothing to do now but stare out the window at the barren scenery and hope that eventually someone would show up to get her back to civilization. *What a beautifully appropriate metaphor for my life,* she thought bitterly. Trapped in desolation, forced to wait for a rescue that might never come.

She was on her way home from Jack Powell's apartment, and she was already in a foul mood. Without apology, Powell had informed her that the little love nest they'd planned for their vacation would have to be put on hold for a few days, as he went off into the mountains, chaperoning the school ski trip. He'd forbidden her to come along—not that she'd wanted to. He was afraid of what she might do if they were in public together. As if she had no self-control.

Kaia had plenty of control—enough, at least, not to show him how disappointed she was. How repulsed she was by the thought of spending her winter break in Grace, sitting in her big, empty house, staring at the tasteful taupe walls. If Powell wanted to pretend he didn't need her around, she could do the same.

The sun had just dipped below the horizon, and the pink desert sunset was swiftly fading to a deep and dark night sky. Kaia shivered with a sudden chill and wondered what might be out there, in that empty stretch of land that lay beyond the road. Seventeen years in New York City had taught her an important safety lesson: Dark and isolated equals danger. Her flight instinct was difficult to suppress.

Not that she expected some drug-crazed mugger to pop out from behind the scrub brush—but still, it was dark and quiet, and she was miles away from civilization. If you could call it that. Her father had once told her there were jackals and coyotes roaming the land—and she'd seen enough cheesy horror movies to at least wonder what else might be out there, lying in wait.

Kaia could take care of herself. She'd had plenty of experience, hadn't she? It's not like anyone had ever looked out for her, or let her believe there was someone ready to catch her when she fell. But fending off a crazed pervert on the subway—or a crazed ex-boyfriend in a high school parking lot—was one thing. Being stranded, isolated, helpless? That was another.

Still, she sat motionless in the car, posing for an invisible audience, calm, cool, and collected. She didn't call someone, anyone, just for the comfort of the sound of another human voice. She didn't wrap her fingers around the steering wheel with a white-knuckled grip, and she didn't whirl her head around at the slightest sound or movement coming from just beyond her peripheral vision. And when the tow truck finally arrived, an hour later, she didn't crack a smile.

Especially not when she recognized the driver. It was that slacker from school, that scuzzy, stoned, frustratingly sexy guy who lately seemed to show up everywhere she turned. He wore a grease-stained T-shirt and oversize jeans with a gaping hole at the left knee, and as he hopped out of the truck and loped toward her, Kaia noted with disgust that his shoes were held together with duct tape. His scruffy black hair was crying out for shampoo, and his face was covered with dark stubble—five o'clock shadow, maybe, but from which day? This was her conquering hero: tall, dark, and dirty.

"Took you long enough," she grumbled as he helped her into the cab of the tow truck.

"Nice to see you again, too, Kaia," he said, checking one last time that the BMW was firmly attached to the back of the truck and then climbing into the driver's seat.

"Do I know you?" she asked, wrinkling her nose to make it clear that an acquaintanceship with his type seemed unlikely.

"You've seen me around," he grunted.

Nice of him not to bring up the time he'd rescued her from some drunken barfly looking for a new floozy for his harem. Kaia had done her best to forget. But now to be rescued yet again by the same deadbeat? It was bringing all the sordid details rushing back. Not that she was ready to offer her thanks. Or even her acknowledgment.

Instead, Kaia snapped her fingers as if she'd just made the connection.

"You're the pizza guy!" she said triumphantly. "Weed, wasn't it?"

"Reed." He shook his head and scowled. "Reed Sawyer."

"Of course, of course. Can't imagine what made me think of weed." *Could it be the stench of pot following you around everywhere you go?* she added silently.

"Maybe it's because you keep tossing me away and I just keep coming back," he suggested, seeming to take cheer from her discomfort.

"So you drive a tow truck now?" she asked. As if she cared.

"It's my dad's garage. I help him out sometimes."

A grease monkey? It figured.

They drove in silence for a while, Kaia doing her best not to admire the way his sinewy body moved beneath the grungy black T-shirt and decaying jeans.

Such a shame, a prize specimen like this, buried beneath so much grime. *But if I cleaned him up a little* . . . she mused—then caught herself in horror. Now was *not* the time to be taking in a stray. No matter how his taut, tan forearm brushed her skin as he shifted gears, no matter how firmly his long, thin fingers massaged the steering wheel, no matter how—*stop*, she warned herself. *Just stop.*

"So, you okay?" he finally asked.

"Why wouldn't I be?"

"I pick up a lot of women out here," he explained. "Being alone, stranded for all that time in the middle of nowhere, it drives 'em crazy. By the time I get there, they're usually pretty shaken up."

"And I guess when they see you and that sexy smile of yours, they just fall into your arms, swooning with gratitude," she sneered. Her voice quivered as he turned his head briefly toward her. She ignored it. "Yours for the taking—is that what you're waiting for?"

"I'm waiting for a thank-you," he answered, unruffled. "But if you're in a swooning mood . . ."

"Thank you," she said grudgingly, turning to stare out the dusty window and watch the shadowy scenery fly by.

"You're welcome." There was a pause, and then, "So, I've got a sexy smile?"

Damn.

"Forget it," Kaia snapped. "I guess you desert cowboys are as unfamiliar with sarcasm as you are with personal hygiene."

She didn't turn back to face him, and he didn't say anything, but she could imagine the superior look on his face, the mocking smile.

And, for the record, it was sexier than ever.

✧✧✧

Adam pulled into the lot and hopped out of his car. He was late. He'd wanted to greet Harper as soon as she'd finished her first shift. But the coach had kept him after practice to work on his free throws.

"You seem off today," the coach had observed.

Wonder why.

Now he jogged toward the entrance—he hated making her wait.

But the figure standing in the entryway anxiously scanning the parking lot wasn't Harper, it was Beth. A fact that he registered only moments before sweeping her into his arms.

Instead, he stopped short, and gave a halfhearted wave. She offered him a weak smile.

"Picking up Harper?" she asked, and he wondered whether she, too, was suddenly remembering all the moments they'd shared in this doorway, Adam rescuing her from a long night of work.

He nodded.

"She's getting changed," Beth told him, refusing to meet his eyes.

"Thanks. And . . . I guess you're waiting for . . ."

"Kane. Yeah." She looked over his shoulder into the parking lot again, as if willing the Camaro to appear. It didn't.

"So anyway, how's—"

"Adam, I wanted to—"

They spoke at once, then stopped abruptly and laughed.

"Well, this is awkward," Beth admitted.

"Tell me about it." Adam idly rubbed the back of his neck. Where was Harper? "Maybe I should just go inside and—"

"Adam, wait." She put her hand on his arm to stop him, then snatched it back—they both froze. It was the first time she'd touched him since . . . since the last time he'd pushed her away. He'd forgotten how soft her hands were. "Adam, there's something I've been really wanting to say to you. I know you think that—"

She broke off, and he waited, wondering. It was the first time in a long time he'd been able to look at her without flinching, without needing to turn away or worse, to hurt her. Did this mean he was finally getting over her? It certainly felt like he was getting over . . . something.

"Well . . . ," she began again hesitantly, "I want you to know that, even after everything that's—"

"Adam!" Pushing past Beth, Harper came flying into his arms. "So sorry I'm late. You have no idea what kind of a day I had."

He gently extricated himself from her embrace and took her hand. "You can tell me all about it in the car, Harper. I'm sure you did great in there today."

Harper gave him a kiss on the cheek and then put a possessive arm around his shoulders.

"Oh, I couldn't have done it without Beth," she gushed, smiling at Beth, whose face had begun to pale. "I can't wait to tell you what a wonderful *help* she was today."

Adam glanced quickly over at Harper, unable to tell whether she was sincere. It wasn't like her to have anything so nice to say about anyone, much less Beth.

I never give her enough credit, he chided himself. He'd

have to make sure that tonight, at least, he told her how proud he was of her. Not just for the job, but for everything.

Feeling a sudden rush of warmth and gratitude that he had someone like Harper in his life, Adam pulled her into a hug and gave her a long kiss.

"What was that for?" she asked when they finally broke apart.

"Just because," he said sheepishly, keeping his arms around her.

"He does that *all* the time," Harper explained to Beth, who couldn't even muster a smile. "Oh, but I guess you, of all people, know that!"

"Hey, were you about to say something?" Adam asked, remembering they'd been interrupted. For a moment, he'd almost forgotten Beth was there.

"No, it was nothing," Beth mumbled. "You guys have a good night."

Harper and Adam walked off toward the car together, hand in hand. Halfway there, he turned back. Beth's solitary figure seemed suddenly frail and lonely, standing in the shadows.

"You sure you'll be okay here?" he called back. "You don't need a ride or anything?"

"I'm fine," she shouted, with just a hint of a quaver in her voice. "Kane will be here any minute."

That's right—Kane. Beth was his problem now, Adam reminded himself. He knew that. It was just that looking at her there, her blond hair billowing around her head like a golden halo, it was a little too easy to forget.

It had been one of the worst days of her life—which made the night that much sweeter. After driving home, they'd come out back to lie together under the stars, on the large, flat rock between the border of their two backyards. It had been a long and painful day, and all she wanted to do was lie in his arms and breathe him in. Unfortunately, Adam had other ideas.

"Can you believe Kane? Grinning at me like that? As if nothing had ever happened?"

Harper sighed and rolled toward Adam, wrapping her arms around him.

"Maybe you should try not to think about it so much," she suggested. "I hate to see you like this."

"I can't stand it!" Adam raged. "I mean, what does she even see in him?"

Harper just clung to him tighter and tried to ignore his words and their meaning. They had never really talked about what had happened between Adam and Beth, and Harper liked it that way. Because that way she could pretend that he'd forgotten. Moved on. That he only cared about Harper and what she wanted.

"He's been with so many women," Adam continued. "He's a slut, you know? Can a guy be a slut? Because he is—and she just fell for it. Like he'll treat her any better than the rest of them." He snorted. "Someone like that will never change."

Almost unnoticeably, Harper stiffened and pulled away. It was that word. *Slut.* Not that she thought she—or that Adam—saw her as—

The thing was, Harper was no vestal virgin. She didn't regret any of the things she'd done—even if she had, she could never take them back. She'd never be Beth—and if that's what he wanted . . .

"Hey, where are you going?" Adam asked, finally noticing that she was slowly easing away from him. He placed a warm hand on her cheek and grazed his fingers down her neck. "I'm sorry, I shouldn't be talking about this. It's not fair to you."

"No." She sat up, pulling him up next to her, and took both of his hands in hers. "I want you to talk about whatever you need to. You can say anything to me. You know that."

He gave her a mischievous smile. "Does that mean I'm allowed to call you 'Gracie' as much as I want?" he asked, knowing how much she hated the childhood nickname.

"Only if I'm allowed to tickle you as much as *I* want!" she shot back, and launched herself at him, wrestling him onto his back as he shook with laughter. Finally, she took pity on him and quieted him with a long, deep kiss. It went on and on—and though she'd promised herself that she would wait just a bit longer, until they were up in the mountains, away, alone, and everything was perfect, she didn't want to pull away. His lips were so soft, his kiss so firm, and their bodies felt so right together, as if each had been designed with the other in mind.

So, after several long minutes, it was Adam who pulled away first, breathless. He brushed a lock of hair away from her face and kissed her lightly on the forehead. It was a cold, clear night, and as she lay against the cool granite, she could see her dark bedroom window. How many nights had she come home alone and gazed out at the backyard, at the rock where she and Adam used to play as children, wishing she were out there with him again? And how many of those nights had he been in his own room, only a few yards away—with Beth?

"Harper, I just want you to know," Adam murmured softly in her ear, "I love—"

Her heart stopped beating.

"—being here with you," he concluded.

She closed her eyes for a moment, then opened them slowly, gazing into his clear, trusting eyes. So he loved . . . being with her.

It wasn't everything—but it was a beginning.

chapter

4

Adam had been waiting desperately for the chance to get away from everything, to clear his head. It had been such a confusing autumn, everything falling apart so suddenly, the world he thought he knew turning upside down. He just wanted to get away from it all: the classes, the pressure, the people. He was hoping he and Harper could have a long, quiet, romantic weekend to figure everything out, to be together, leave school and all that baggage behind.

But that's the thing about school trips: the rest of the school has a nasty habit of coming along.

"Dude, I am going to *tear* up those slopes!"

Which is, Adam supposed, how he'd ended up stuffed in the back of a school bus with a bunch of his basketball "buddies" listening to them vie for the title of BMOC (Big Moron Off Campus).

"There better be some hot honeys up there!"

"Yeah, because I'm looking for a ski bunny who knows

all about going down—and I *don't* mean down the mountain!"

"Good one, man."

It's not that he didn't like hanging out with the guys—even now, as they were bragging about their nonexistent ski skills and carving their initials into the cracked leather bus seats—but he just wasn't in the mood.

"What's the matter, Morgan?" his seatmate asked, elbowing him in the ribs. "All this guy talk too rough for you? You'd rather be up front with the ladies?"

Uh—yes?

"This dude is so whipped," his first-string point guard confided to the rest of the team. They roared in approval.

"Like you'd be talking about the honeys if Nikki was back here," Adam shot back, and the point guard shut up, fast. He could intimidate 6'4" guys on the court—but 5'3" Nikki left him quivering in his Nikes, and they all knew it. When the girls were around, everyone clammed up, like perfect gentlemen.

But the girls were all the way up in the front of the bus, the guys had slipped some Baileys into their morning coffee—and the desert road stretched ahead of them with no end in sight.

"I'm gonna get so ripped tonight—you guys in?"

"Shit, yeah!"

Adam smiled weakly as his teammates cheered around him.

His inner five-year-old had only one silent, but increasingly insistent question: *Are we there yet?*

Not even close.

Winter in the desert sucked.

Kaia knew she shouldn't have been too surprised—
everything in the desert sucked—but winter was yet
another, surprisingly painful disappointment.

She'd always looked forward to the season with a childlike enthusiasm: skating in Rockefeller Center, Frozen Hot
Chocolate at Serendipity, the Macy's Christmas decorations, even *The Nutcracker* at Lincoln Center. By January,
everyone would be tired of the biting cold, the dark skies,
the ever-present slush. But in December, winter was fresh
and new, the air crisp and refreshing, and it was as if the
entire city came alive.

Here, on the other hand—nothing. More hot days,
more cold nights. Desert wind, desert sand. No ice skating,
no cozy Burberry scarves—and certainly, no snow.

She'd called Powell, hoping that even from a distance
he could liven up her night. But there'd been no answer.
And he hadn't called back. Not that Kaia missed him. Not
that she wished she was up there on a stupid school trip—
even home was an improvement over that. (Having her
teeth drilled during a Novocain shortage would have been
an improvement over that.) But she was bored, and she was
bitter. And she couldn't ignore the fact that while she was
stuck on the couch, Powell would be whooshing his way
down the slopes. And he wouldn't be alone. That handsome
figure and sexy accent pretty much went to waste in a
town like Grace; a ski resort, however, was a whole different story.

Not that Kaia cared. She had a life of her own—even
if it wasn't a very thrilling one at the moment.

On a sudden impulse, she grabbed the phone book and

flipped open to the entry for Guido's Pizza. She wasn't that hungry—especially not for the dried-out slab covered in greasy processed cheese and a watery layer of sauce that Guido had the nerve to call "pizza." But if the pizza wasn't tasty, the delivery boy definitely was—and, hungry or not, Kaia could use some good eye candy.

Let Powell do whatever he wanted up on the mountain. She was more than ready to have a little fun of her own.

"You're going down!" Harper squealed, as Adam mashed a handful of snow down the back of her jacket.

The school had done a surprisingly decent job of picking a resort. White Stone Lodge was no prize in itself. The bus was parked in front of a complex of stout, reddish residential buildings all circling the three-story main lodge building, covered with faux brick and stone in a failed attempt to make it look homey. But even a run-down Motel 6 would have looked appealing in such a setting—a glistening blanket of snow covered the roofs, and delicate icicles dangled over the edge, turning the lodge into a giant gingerbread house rimmed with dripping sugar crystals. Jagged mountain peaks loomed in the background, slicing through a storybook blue sky. The endless grayish beige of the flat desert landscape had never seemed so far away.

Adam raced away as Harper scooped up an armful of snow and sent it flying in his direction.

"Face it, you suck at this, Gracie!" he called from a safe distance, pegging a snowball in her direction.

Oh, really?

She scooped up another handful and raced after him,

tackling him to the ground. They tumbled into the snow together, heaving with laughter. Adam rolled over her and held a dripping snowball a few inches from her face.

"You want a piece of me?" he asked in a mock threatening voice, as icy drops spattered down on her.

She looked up at his flushed face, illuminated by a childlike joy, and suddenly lifted her head up to kiss him.

"I want *all* of you," she said sincerely—and then, before he could stop her, grabbed the hand with the snowball and smashed it into his face.

"You snooze, you lose," she crowed, exploding into laughter. He fell to the ground beside her, laughing just as hard.

The sky looked so different up here, she thought, barely noticing the chill creeping through her fingers and toes. It seemed so much closer, as if she could reach up and grab a cloud.

Adam's gloved hand took her own, and she snuggled against him, wishing that they weren't sprawled out in the open behind the resort. She wanted to be alone with him—now.

"Think your roommate's going to be around tonight?" she asked innocently. Harper hadn't actually told Adam about her WFS plan, but she figured he would see the possibilities of this weekend just as clearly as she did.

"Nah, Nikki kicked out her roommate, so he's not going to be coming back tonight."

Or ever, Harper thought—once Nikki got her claws into someone, she was unlikely to let go.

"So if you wanted to," Adam began again, tentatively.

"It would be a shame to let an empty room go to

waste," she said casually. But her heart was thudding in her ears. Why was she so nervous?

"Are you sure?" he asked—and there was nothing casual about his tone.

She looked around at the sky, the mountains, the snow—his face. It was the perfect spot for a perfect moment.

"I'm sure."

Since their chaperone had disappeared within minutes of arrival, the Haven High kids were free to do whatever they wanted at White Stone Lodge. There was a party in room 17, free pot in room 32, and Miranda was pretty sure she'd heard something about skinny-dipping in the hot tub.

But Miranda wasn't in the mood. She'd brought along her new, über-portable laptop in hopes there'd be some kind of wireless network she could tap into. Her dating profile had been up for a few days and, much as she hated to admit it, she was desperate to see whether anyone had responded to her. It seemed a little pathetic, to have come all this way, spent all this money, just to spend another Saturday night at home in front of the computer . . . but on the other hand, she thought, logging on to her e-mail server, Harper was likely gone for the night, so it's not like anyone would ever have to know.

Congratulations, **Spitfire**, the following **3** users have expressed interest in your profile!
User Profile: TheDude
Sex: male
Age: 17

Height: 6'1"
Favorite color: gold
Favorite food: beer
If I were an animal, I'd be: a PARTY animal
Celebrity I most look like: Brad Pitt
Best lie I've ever told: No Officer, I haven't been drinking.
Three things I can't live without: beer, sex, pot
I am . . . one wild and crazy guy, looking to party it up with one (or more) lucky ladies.
You are . . . totally hot, especially in a miniskirt—and out of one. If you know what I mean. Wink, wink.

And then there was bachelor number two . . .

User Profile: HanSolo
Sex: male
Age: 16
Height: 5'3 1/2"
Favorite color: Martian red
Favorite food: peanuts
If I were an animal, I'd be: a Wookie
Best lie I've ever told: It's not a doll—it's an action figure.
Celebrity I most look like: Mark Hamill
Three things I can't live without: *Star Wars* boxed set, comic books, and my scale model of the Millennium Falcon (I built it myself!)
I am . . . the guy at the back of the class that you've never noticed before. The one lurking by

your locker that you brush past without a word. I'm very smart, I just need some help with my people skills—at least that's what my mom says.

You are . . . friendly, nice, a *Star Wars* fan (may the Force be with you!). You like going to conventions and building models. And you would be willing to dress up like Princess Leia in the gold bikini.

And, of course, Miranda's personal favorite:

User Profile: Thrasher
Sex: Yes, please
Age: 18
Height: 11 inches
Favorite color: whatever color your thong is
Favorite food: pizza
If I were an animal, I'd be: a coyote
Best lie I've ever told: Of course I remember your name.
Celebrity I most look like: the Rock
Three things I can't live without: my bike, my booze, my band
I am . . . a guy who likes motorcycles, trucks, booze, and hard rock.

You are . . . a chick who digs guys who like motorcycles, trucks, booze, and hard rock.

Spitfire, if you would like to send a message to any of these users, click here.

Miranda snorted in disgust. What had she been thinking? Like anyone other than the freaks and the geeks would be using this stupid Web site. She could only imagine the look on these losers' faces if they ever saw who they'd picked. There was a horrifying thought: Even these freak shows probably wouldn't want to date her if they got the chance.

Face it, Miranda, she told herself, flicking off the computer. *You're just doomed to be alone—forever.*

"We should really get some sleep," Beth pointed out, wriggling out of Kane's grasp.

He checked the clock on the nightstand: 10:40.

"Sleep?" he asked in surprise. "It's way too early for that. Besides"—he grabbed her and pulled her down beside him—"I'm sure we can find something more interesting to do."

She stiffened beneath his grasp and, again, pulled away.

Kane issued a silent curse—pulling away was all she ever did, and this whole chase thing was beginning to lose its luster. "Fine, we'll sleep," he said irritably. "I've been looking forward to waking up next to you—"

"Actually," she interrupted, rising from the bed and pulling on her shirt (despite his best efforts, her jeans had never even made it off), "I think I should go back to my room."

"Why? We've got plenty of space, plenty of privacy. Isn't this why we—?"

She bit her lip and nervously tucked her hair behind her ears. "We'd get in a lot of trouble if we got caught," she said softly, backing away. "And I should really—besides, it's a big day tomorrow. And maybe tomorrow night . . ."

"Hey, hey, slow down," he urged her, following her to

the door and taking hold of her waist before she slipped out. "What's wrong?" he asked, gently turning her to face him. "You're trembling."

He felt her muscles clench, and for a second he thought she would pull away again, but then she relaxed into the embrace and touched his face lightly with the palm of her hand. "I just need to go," she told him. "Okay?"

"Of course it's okay," he promised.

"You're not mad?"

"Not mad at all." He kissed her, softly and gently, breathing her in. "But are you sure?"

"You make it pretty hard to be sure," she told him, pressing against him and kissing him again, with more urgency this time, gripping his body as if it were a life preserver, keeping her afloat. "*Really* hard."

There was more kissing.

And then she was gone.

"Harper?" he whispered.

The room was dark, and she could see only a bare outline of his figure, carved out by a shaft of moonlight filtering through the window. She pressed herself against him, running her hands across his face, his skin, trying to memorize the shape of his body, the feel of it beneath her fingers.

"Harper, you know I—with Kaia—"

"I know," she said quietly, stopping him with a kiss. The last thing she wanted to hear about, think about, was Kaia. Adam with Kaia. Not here—not now.

"I just want you to know," he pressed on, "it was just

that once—and this is the first time with . . ." He stopped and rolled over on his side, his face inches from hers. He brushed a lock of hair away from her eyes. "It's different with you."

"Adam, you don't have to do this. We can just—"

"No, I need to say this," he told her, "before we—I need you to know that . . . how much I . . . I've never known anyone like you, Harper. You're the only person in my life I can always count on—"

"You know I'll always be there for you," she reminded him. "Believe me."

"I believe everything you say, Gracie, because I know you're the one person who always tells me the truth. Promise me you always will."

"Oh, Adam . . ." She grabbed him then and kissed him, hard, wrapping his arms around her and pressing herself against his bare skin. She was done talking. And it was a good thing—because the next words out of her mouth would have been a lie.

"Yo, dude, you in there?"

The loud voice was quickly followed by a pounding on the door and some raucous laughter. Harper quickly rolled away from him, and Adam groaned in frustration. The guys. Great. Their timing was just impeccable.

"Go away!" Adam shouted, grabbing his sneaker off the floor and throwing it toward the door. "I'm busy."

"*Getting* busy is more like it," another voice called out.

"Asses," Adam muttered. He turned toward Harper in apology. "Just give me a second and I'll deal with this," he promised, eager to get back to what they'd barely started.

"You know what?" she gave him a quick peck on the lips and hopped out of bed, pulling the sheet around herself. "Let me."

Harper strode toward the door, but froze midway there when the shouting started up again.

"You got Grace in there, dude?"

"She'll show you a *good* time—and I should know!"

"You got me to thank, bro. I taught her everything she knows."

"Just don't hog her. Leave some for the rest of us!"

Adam leaped out of bed and stormed past Harper, flinging open the door.

"Get the hell out of here," he growled, leveling a fist at the cluster of grinning idiots.

"Dude, chill, we're just having some fun with you."

"Fun's over," he said shortly, and swung the door shut in their faces. "They're drunk," he told Harper, feeling like he needed to apologize, as if this were all somehow his fault. "Come on," he urged her. She was still standing frozen in the middle of the floor. "Let's go back to bed."

They climbed onto the soft mattress and swaddled themselves in the downy comforter, and Adam again took her in his arms.

"Ad, those things they said," Harper began hesitantly, in a tentative and unfamiliar voice.

"Shh, it doesn't matter," he promised her. "Nothing's changed—we're still here, together. I still want you."

And he did, desperately.

But he couldn't stop hearing their words, their laughter. He couldn't focus. And as he eased himself on top of her, ready to take their relationship to the next level, to start them off on a new beginning, he discovered—to his horror and humiliation—that he just couldn't.

Kane closed the door softly behind Beth—then gave it a sharp kick for good measure. What had been the point of finagling the single room? Of talking her into coming in the first place? For God's sake, it wasn't even eleven o'clock yet—was he supposed to just be a good boy and go to sleep?

Calm down, he told himself. He didn't like exposing too much of his emotions, even in private. He was nothing without his poker face, and practice made perfect.

Speaking of poker . . .

He'd overheard some of the staff talking about a weekly poker game, and had no doubt he could talk himself into it.

He weighed his options.

Sleep? Not so much an option as a failure.

Partying with his peers in some smoky, overcrowded room that, by this point, probably had sweat on the walls and vomit on the floor? Kane didn't associate with these losers when they were in town—and he saw no reason to make an exception for their change in zip code.

Poker it was.

He crept through the lounge on his way to the staff quarters, wary of running into their absentee chaperone.

Turns out his instincts were half right: Jack Powell *was* in the lounge, but judging from the blonde precariously balanced on his lap, nibbling his ear, he wasn't going to be doing much chaperoning anytime soon.

Kane shook his head in admiration—finally, a member

of the Haven High teaching staff he could look up to.

Newly inspired, he went off in search of some fun of his own. Not *too* much fun, he reminded himself. After all, he had a girlfriend now—a real one. And that meant no extracurricular activities. If Adam could do it, he could do it.

As he'd suspected, his charm was more than enough to get him admitted to the back room and then to the poker game—though he supposed waving around a ready wad of cash hadn't hurt.

It had been just what he'd expected: dark room, good Scotch, and two beautiful women facing him across the table. Those compact, svelte bodies, hard muscles only highlighting the soft curves . . . There was only one surprise. Sitting to the right of Amber and Claire was a more familiar face: Harper.

"What are you doing here?" Kane asked, taking a seat at the makeshift poker table.

Harper rolled her eyes. "Don't ask. And you?"

"I'd say that's a good policy. Don't ask and"—Kane glanced at the buxom brunette on his right and the luscious blonde on his left—"don't tell."

"Your deal," said the guy who'd let him into the game, handing him the cards. "Oh, and did Amber tell you?"

"Did Amber tell me what?" Kane asked, winking at her.

"We usually play a warm-up round before we start tossing the money around," Amber explained. "Just to get us in the mood. Strip poker." She looked him up and down. "I hope you don't mind."

"Mind?" He glanced toward Harper, who only smiled and raised an eyebrow. "Trust me, I don't mind at all."

❖❖❖

Was she crazy?

Kaia stared out the dusty window of the pickup truck, wondering if she'd lost her mind. What other excuse could there be for her agreeing to this ridiculous plan?

A few hours earlier, as she'd half hoped and half feared, Reed had shown up with her cold, greasy pizza. After trading yet another round of insults, she'd challenged him to find some way to alleviate her Grace-induced boredom. He, in turn, had shown up at the end of his shift with a dirty pickup truck and a challenge of his own: Drive off into the middle of nowhere with a skuzzy stranger and hope that his definition of "something interesting to do" wouldn't land her in the morgue.

She didn't even know why she'd called him. So he was hot. Fine. There was no point in denying that. Nor could she deny the fact that when he looked at her, when his eyes burned into her, she trembled.

But that was irrelevant. It had to be. Kaia Sellers could *not* involve herself with someone like this *Weed*, poor, stupid, aimless, and completely unacceptable. Couldn't, and wouldn't. And yet . . .

And yet, she'd made the call. And when he'd shown up at her door, she'd welcomed him in, hadn't she? Leaned toward him, so he would smell her perfume. Favored him with a sultry smile.

And now here she was in the old truck, Reed by her side, speeding through the darkened landscape, the lights of civilization (if Grace qualified) fading into the distance behind them.

I must be crazy, Kaia thought, unsure whether to be appalled or amused. It was the only possible explanation.

Crazy was fine—for a night. But whatever happened, Kaia promised herself, one night was all it would ever be. Reed Sawyer could not be allowed into her life. He didn't fit. And never would.

They drove in silence, and when the truck suddenly came to a stop, Reed turned off the engine and got out without a word. Kaia climbed out as well (once it became painfully clear he wasn't planning on opening the door for her) and looked around in dismay. If this wasn't the *middle* of nowhere, surely it was only a stone's throw away.

That's it—he brought me here to kill me, she thought in sudden alarm.

They were parked on the shoulder of a dusty road that stretched across the flat land until it disappeared into the darkness. Ahead of them sat the massive, hulking frame of a gutted industrial complex, long since abandoned.

"We're *here*?" she asked, masking her increasing panic with the comfortably familiar cloak of disdain.

He nodded, and hopped up on the hood of the truck.

"And where is 'here,' exactly?"

"This is Grace Mines," he explained. "Or used to be. It closed down—then it burned down."

"And then what?" she asked, intrigued in spite of herself. She hopped up onto the hood of the truck next to him, looking more closely at the shattered remains of the mine, gleaming in the light of the full moon.

"Then nothing. Who has the money to do anything about it?" he asked rhetorically. "It's been like this ever since I can remember. I guess it always will be."

Kaia tried to imagine the empty husk before her as it had been in the boom times, teeming with workers, young men seeking their fortune, fathers struggling to support their families, the air filled with the clicking and whirring of machinery. This place had been alive once. And now? Weeds sprouted amid the fallen beams, empty beer cans lay strewn in piles of ash, the jagged glass of the shattered windows splintered the moonlight—now, it was just a corpse. A fallen giant, a dead zone, soon to be reclaimed by the wilderness around it.

"You come here often?" she asked, her tone more serious than she'd intended.

He nodded. "Something about it—" He looked over at her, then looked away. "We can go, if you want."

"No, I want to stay for a while."

And she was surprised to discover it was true.

They sat there side by side, not talking, not touching. They sat for a long time, just staring at the old building, at the desert that lay beyond it. Kaia shivered once and, wordlessly, Reed tucked his jacket around her shoulders. It was heavy and warm—and smelled like him. Not pot this time, but a deep, rich scent, like dark coffee by an open fire. It fit here—*he* fit here—strange and dark, like the ruins, with a quiet dignity.

She was about to take his hand when she felt the first spatter of rain.

Rain? In the desert?

Before she had time to be confused, the skies opened up. It was as if bucket after bucket of icy water were being dumped from above—the rain fell fast and hard, pelting their skin, turning the desert dirt around them into rivers of mud.

"What the hell is this?" Kaia complained as they both scrambled back into the truck. "It's not supposed to rain in the desert!"

"Sometimes it does," he said simply, hoisting her into the passenger seat, then rushing around to the driver's side, finally throwing himself in and slamming the door.

They looked at each other—both sopping wet, their hair and clothes plastered to their bodies—and burst into laughter.

"This is, by far, the weirdest date I've ever had," Kaia said, wringing out the edge of her shirt as best she could.

"Who says it's a date?" he retorted, but with a smile.

"We should probably wait for it to let up before we drive home," Kaia said, gesturing toward the opaque sheet of water flooding down the windshield.

"I guess we should," he agreed. "Cold?"

"What?"

"You're shivering."

She was cold, she realized. She hadn't noticed. She nodded and, hesitantly, he put an arm around her. She inched to the left, resting herself against him. It wasn't much warmer—but she stayed.

She leaned her head against his shoulder and they listened to the rain pelting the truck, spattering against the soft ground. She shivered again, and he held her tighter. His wet hair was still dripping, and she watched the drops of water trace their way down his face. They looked like tears.

They sat there together, motionless, for a long time.

And then the rain stopped. And they drove away.

chapter

5

"Beth, did you really think I'd be coming to ski school with you?" Kane asked, laughing.

She blushed and shook her head. "That was silly. I guess I thought maybe you'd teach me—"

He snapped her ski boot shut and helped her latch it to the ski, then grabbed his board and began guiding her toward the bunny slope.

Kane laughed again. "Me? Only if you want to land in the hospital. Trust me, you don't want to pick up any of my bad habits."

The hospital?

Beth's heart plummeted as she pictured herself in a broken heap at the bottom of a snow-covered cliff.

"It's going to be fine," Kane assured her, catching her look of terror. "I just want you to learn from the best. This way, I can get some good boarding in—and then we'll have all afternoon to spend together."

"Okay," she agreed. She leaned over to try to give him

a quick kiss through his ski mask, and practically toppled over into the snow. "And Kane?" she asked as he steadied her. "I'm sorry again about last night."

"No apology necessary. And I'm glad I got the chance to go to bed early, for once. You were right—we have a big day ahead of us!" he said heartily, and with that, he grinned and glided away, waving in farewell as he careened down the slope.

Beth took a deep breath and inched her way toward the sign marked WHITE STONE SKI SCHOOL: BUNNY BEGINNERS. If she was having this much trouble on flat land, she wasn't too eager to find out how she would fare on the slopes. But she supposed she didn't really have another option.

Beth took a place next to Miranda, the only person in the lesson she recognized. They exchanged a quick glance—the disappointed *Oh, it's you* vibe was palpable.

But there was little time for disappointment or hostility, not when the instructor, a chipper young woman in a fluorescent orange ski suit and matching skis, had already started rattling off instructions at lightning speed.

Knees locked, knees bent. Shift your weight. But not too much. Hold your balance. Ski poles down. Arms out—

It was far more than Beth could take in, and by the time the instructor began offering tips for slowing down, Beth was half ready to throw her ski poles off the mountain and spend the rest of the day reading in the lodge. Somehow, the instructor's suggestions—"Line up your skis like french fries to go fast"; "Angle your skis like a slice of pizza to go slow"—didn't inspire her with much confidence that, when plummeting down the hill toward a giant tree, she'd be able to avoid it.

"Okay, bunnies, time for our first run!" the instructor cheered. "Just push off—and . . . go!"

As the students around her launched themselves into motion, Beth looked dubiously over the lip of the so-called bunny slope. It suddenly looked like a ninety-degree angle.

"You have *got* to be kidding me," Miranda muttered under her breath. She looked about as confident in her abilities as Beth felt.

After a moment, they were the only two students left at the top of the hill. Miranda gave Beth a half smile.

"It's going to be pretty embarrassing if we give up now, isn't it?" she asked sheepishly.

"Embarrassment never killed anyone," Beth pointed out, "whereas skiing . . ." It was a *long* way down.

"On the count of three?" Miranda suggested.

Beth nodded and, hesitantly, quietly, they counted off together.

One.

Two.

Threeeeeeeee . . .

I'm not going to die, Beth repeated to herself aloud as she hurtled uncontrollably down the hill. The wind whipped past her face, the bumpy ground skidding beneath her feet.

French fries. Pizza. French fries—no, pizza, she mumbled to herself, trying to force her skis into the proper angle, whatever that was. But it was no use—her skis were going wherever they wanted to go. She was just along for the ride.

It seemed to take forever—then, suddenly, miraculously, she was zooming toward the bottom of the slope, toward a crowd of waiting skiers, unable to stop or turn, snow flying from her wake, until finally, in desperation, she spread her skis into the widest angle she could and slowed to a stop, tumbling over into a blessedly soft mound of snow.

Alive. And safe. And totally ready to do it all over again.

"What a rush!" Miranda cried from a few feet away. She too was flat on her back in the snow, one ski lying by her side, but her face was flushed with happiness.

"A few more runs and we'll be ready for the Olympics," Beth boasted, in a still shaky voice.

Miranda, having picked herself up, offered Beth a hand. "A few *thousand* more runs, maybe," Miranda corrected her. "I don't know about you, but I thought I was going to die pretty much the whole way down."

"I've never been so happy to stop moving in my life," Beth admitted.

"So . . . you ready to go again?"

"Again?" Beth brushed some snow off her face and planted her ski poles defiantly into the snow as if staking a flag into the ground of a newly discovered land. "What are we waiting for!"

"Are you *sure* you don't want to try a lesson first?" Adam asked again.

At least he's talking to me, Harper thought. It was a small but crucial step in the right direction, given that their morning had consisted largely of Adam refusing to meet her gaze. When he'd had to ask her to pass the salt over the cafeteria breakfast table, he'd first turned bright red, stuttered a few incoherent syllables, and finally spit the words out only by looking fixedly down at his lap. Suffice it to say, they hadn't spoken yet about the equipment malfunction of the night before. Fine with Harper. She was more than happy to put the episode far behind her. And judging from the look on his face after it had happened, when she'd tried comforting him ("Don't worry, it happens to everyone"), he was eager to do the same.

The thing was: It didn't happen to everyone. Or, at least, not everyone who was with Harper. No one had ever had any problems in that department when it came to her—so what was going on with Adam? Was there some part of him, deep down, that didn't want to be with her?

Stop obsessing, she told herself. Once they'd gotten out of the lodge and onto the slopes, Adam had relaxed, grateful for the chance to focus on something other than their nonexistent sex life. Harper forced herself to do the same. Unfortunately, that meant focusing on skiing . . . and for Harper, that was proving to be almost as unpleasant a topic.

"Who needs lessons when I've got you?" Harper asked, trying to ignore her clenched stomach and rapid pulse. Their chairlift swung gently in the wind, and Harper grabbed the metal guardrail a little tighter, refusing to look down to the ground below. *Way* below. Instead, she focused on how good the two of them must look together in their ski gear. Harper's shopping expedition had paid off, and she was sporting a svelte, dark green ski jacket with matching ski pants. She looked *good.*

In all her fantasizing about this trip, she'd almost forgotten about the whole skiing component—athletic endeavors were so not her thing. But really, how hard could it be? You just point your skis in the right direction and let gravity do the work. Any idiot could figure that out. She wasn't about to be one of those wimpy bunny slopers that the *real* skiers just laughed at. No one laughed at Harper Grace. Besides, Harper planned to spend the entire day by Adam's side—especially after last night. She didn't want him to spend any time off by himself. Thinking.

The ride ended far too soon, and Adam pushed her off the lift just in time. They paused at the top of the slope. Harper tightened her grip on her ski poles and focused on the little kids zipping back and forth across the mountain—if they could do it, so could she.

"You ready?" Adam asked dubiously.

She nodded.

"You sure?"

She nodded again.

"Just remember what I taught you, okay? And I'll be right behind you the whole way down."

"Don't worry," she assured him. "I'll be fine. . . ."

She pushed herself off down the hill and, suddenly, she was flying through the snow, her hair streaming out behind her, faster and faster. She shifted her weight to the left, to the right, to avoid crashing into someone, veered around an icy patch, and still, faster and faster—

I'm skiing, she marveled, *and I'm* awesome.

And that's when she hit the bump.

And her skis flew up off the ground, taking her with them. She soared through the air, her arms and legs waving wildly, helplessly, and for a moment she felt weightless—and then the ground returned.

With a crash.

A clatter.

A thud.

Silence.

Kane was practically asleep on his feet. Riding down the same beginner trail again and again would have been enough to put anyone into a coma of boredom. And feigning enthusiasm every time Beth made it twenty feet without falling was wearing him out.

"You're doing great," he lied, when they'd landed at the bottom once again. "Think maybe it's time for you to try a more difficult slope?"

"Oh, I don't know." She bit her lip and looked up at the mountain peaks in the distance. "I don't think I'm ready for that yet."

"You're better than you think you are," he prodded her.

She shook her head. "Not that much better."

He shrugged and began maneuvering his snowboard back toward the chairlift. "Whatever—we'll just go again."

She grabbed him and pulled him to a stop, slightly off the trail.

"Kane, if *you* want to go hit some harder slopes for a while, it's okay."

"I'm not going to just leave you here," he protested, imagining himself shooting down a black diamond trail, chasing the wind. It killed him to be out here in such fresh powder, stuck gliding down the same bunny hill over and over again, at snail speed. "But why don't you come along—you're really getting good now."

She laughed. "And what definition of good are you using? No, I'm staying here. But really, you go—have some fun. We'll meet up later."

She was lying, that much was clear. She wanted him with her, and was terrified to ski by herself. He should stay. That would be the good boyfriend move. It would have been Adam's move. *But she's not with Adam,* he reminded himself. And who knew *what* she really wanted, if she wasn't going to admit it. Why not take her at face value, enjoy himself? It was fresh powder, after all, and a new board. You don't waste that. Not if you're Kane Geary.

"Have I mentioned how beautiful you look out here?" he told her. "Like a snow goddess."

She pushed him playfully. "You don't have to butter me up, Kane. I'm not going to be mad if you go—you came up here to board. You should do it."

"That's not all I came for," he reminded her, pulling her scarf away from her face so he could warm her chilled lips with a kiss.

"Well then, you'd better take care of yourself up there and make sure you stay in one piece . . . so you can meet me later," she told him, with an uncharacteristically mischievous note in her voice. This was working out better than he could have hoped.

"Wouldn't miss it," he assured her.

"And remember—" she called after him as he slid away.

"I'll be careful!" he promised.

But really, what was the fun in that?

Harper didn't know what had been more humiliating. Lying on the ground, snow seeping through her clothes, as more and more curious skiers gathered to gawk? Being strapped to the back of a rescue mobile like a couch strapped to the hood of a car and then unceremoniously unloaded in front of half her school? Or maybe it was the fact that after thoroughly examining her, the doctor at the first aid station had concluded there was nothing wrong with her other than a few bruises and a twisted knee.

Not that she wasn't grateful. Imagine if she'd broken her neck—or, almost as bad, her nose. But the injury was just minor enough to make her feel like an idiot for making such a scene—and just major enough to keep her off her feet for the rest of the weekend.

Adam had tended to her for a while. He was guilt stricken over his abject failure as a ski instructor, and she was only too happy to play his damsel in distress, letting him prop her leg up with pillows, bring her hot chocolate, and kiss her bruises until she had to smile. (And, if nothing else, at least all the commotion had taken his mind off their little "problem.")

He'd been so sweet, in fact, that she'd felt guilty about spoiling his fun. She'd told him to go back out on the slopes—he'd refused, she'd insisted. And finally, he'd given in.

It was only when he'd gone, and she was left alone in the empty lodge, her hot chocolate turned cold, her knee throbbing, the cozy fire burned out, that she realized her stupidity. She was trapped in here, in pain, while Adam was out there alone, easy prey for all those desperate girls who would love nothing more than to steal him away from her.

Easy prey for Beth.

She could see it now.

"Oh, Adam, you look so handsome on your skis!" In that simpering voice. "I'm so sweet and helpless—won't you help me get down the mountain?"

Harper would have been pleased to help her—right over the edge. But Adam, on the other hand, would be nothing but a gentleman, only too happy to lend his services. And once she'd sucked him back in with the needy routine, she'd never let him go.

Kane was nothing, no one, she'd claim. A horrible mistake. Adam was her one, true love.

It was nauseating, even as a hypothetical.

Adam would resist at first. He was nothing if not loyal.

But Beth would beg and Beth would plead—and then, Harper knew, Beth would cry. And she'd look so beautiful and so fragile standing out in the snow, throwing herself on Adam's mercy, that eventually, he would just give in. After all, he would surely reason, Harper's tough, she can handle it. Beth is the one who really needs me.

If only he knew.

It was crazy, she told herself. Totally unlikely—certainly no more likely than a chance meeting in the halls of the high school or the cramped streets of their tiny town. But still, she couldn't stand the idea of Beth out there having *Harper's* dream vacation.

Harper whipped out her cell phone, determined to get her mind off the whole horrible thing. But who to call? Even Miranda was out on the slopes, having fun. Harper was alone. There was only one person she could think of who might have time to talk, distract Harper from her living nightmare—and it wouldn't have been her first choice. Or her fifth. But she was out of options, and sometimes you just had to play the hand you were dealt.

She hit talk.

"Hey, Kaia—yes, it's Harper. Just thought I'd check in, give you the download on the trip so far . . . what? No, nothing too exciting—wait, I *do* have some hot gossip. You'll never guess what our trusty chaperone's been up to. Let's just say he's got his hands full. Or should I say, his lap. . . ."

He didn't notice her until he'd sat down beside her on the chairlift—and by then, it was too late.

This *really* wasn't his day.

They recognized each other at the same time, just as the lift swept their feet off the ground. Now there was no turning back—they were trapped together until they reached the top.

"Hey," Adam grunted.

Beth nodded and looked down. Most of her face was hidden by a thick blue scarf—only her eyes were visible, and he couldn't decipher their expression. Once, he'd been able to read her thoughts, just from the look in her eyes. It felt like a long time ago.

They rode in silence for several long minutes, watching the skiers dart around beneath them. Adam swung his skis, gently rocking them back and forth.

"Could you not do that?" Beth asked. Adam looked over and noticed how tightly she was gripping the guide bar. For a moment, he considered swinging his legs wildly, just to see her face fill with fear. But he suppressed the impulse—and hated himself for it.

"Sorry," he said awkwardly, and stopped. "So, uh, how's the skiing?" *And where's your boyfriend?* he added silently. Nice of Kane to send her off by herself. Typical. But no more than she deserved, he supposed. And she was a big girl. She could handle it.

"It's fine," she responded unconvincingly. "It's great. Kane and I are having a great time."

"It doesn't look it," Adam snapped.

"What?"

"If you two are having such a *great* time together, where is he?"

She looked away. "That's really none of your business," she said bluntly. "Did I ask you where Harper was?"

"She's—"

"I don't care," Beth cut in. "That was my point."

"Fine. Sorry I said anything at all," he retorted.

"Me too."

Beth hopped off the chairlift as soon as her skis could reach the ground. She couldn't get away from Adam fast enough. She hated what being around him did to her. Half the time she was an emotional wreck, ready to throw herself at his feet and beg him to take her back, the other half she was this cold, sarcastic monster she barely recognized.

He deserved it, of course—what right had he to comment on her relationship, act so wise and superior, as if he were just waiting for her and Kane to fall apart? He didn't know anything about them—or anything about her, not anymore.

She was so angry that she forgot to be afraid as she launched herself down the trail. So busy fuming about Adam that she failed to notice the icy patch until it was too late—her legs went skidding out from under her—one ski off to the right, the other off to the left, and just when it felt as if she would snap in half, her skis snapped off instead, and she landed, facefirst, in a pile of snow.

Ouch.

It took her a moment to catch her breath and make sure all her limbs were still attached and in working order. Yes on both counts. She sat up and brushed the snow out of her face, taking stock. One ski lay a few feet away, and there were her two ski poles, but the other ski . . .

Beth's heart sank. It was nowhere in sight. Had it slid down the mountain without her? She wondered how much it would cost to replace a rental ski—and how in the world she'd make it down without it.

"Lose something?"

Adam skied to a stop just in front of her—and he was holding her missing ski.

"I saw it go flying," he explained, "and figured . . . are you okay?"

She nodded and, with some hesitation, took his hand and let him help her up.

"I saw you go flying too," he told her, "and I thought . . ."

"It looked pretty bad, I guess?" she asked with a wry smile.

"No, no," he assured her as she snapped her boots back into the skis. "You were doing great until you fell. You're a natural."

He'd been watching her? Beth felt her face warm, and was glad her scarf would hide the blush. The scarf made her think of Kane—and that made her think it was time to go.

"Well, I guess I should get back on the horse," she said, taking a tentative step forward on the skis, only to topple over once again—and this time, she pulled him down with her.

"I take it back," Adam said, rolling over and spitting out a mouthful of snow. "You totally suck."

He burst into laughter and, after a moment, Beth broke out in giggles.

"I'm so sorry," she gasped, trying to get hold of herself. "Let me help you up."

"No, don't touch me," he warned, but he said it with a warm smile on his face. "I don't want to risk another human avalanche."

He picked himself up and then, again, hoisted her to her feet.

"I guess I should have paid more attention in ski school," Beth admitted ruefully.

Adam flicked a clump of snow off her shoulder, and Beth realized how long it had been since he'd touched her. But just a moment ago he'd grabbed her hand and pulled her upright as if it were nothing.

Which, she supposed, it was.

"I could—I could help you out a little," he suddenly suggested, looking surprised to hear the words pop out of his mouth. He couldn't have been as surprised as Beth.

If he'd asked her ten minutes earlier, she would have laughed in his face. Accept help from Adam? As if.

Suddenly, it didn't seem like such a bad idea. "I guess we could do that," she accepted shyly. "If you want."

"Okay, then," he said, in his can-do voice. She knew it well. But then, she knew everything about him, every inch of him, well. Or, at least, she had. "The first thing we need to do is work on your stopping skills. Did they tell you in your lesson about 'making a pizza'?"

Beth rolled her eyes. "Not you too! I still don't understand what skiing has to do with fast food. It's so ridiculous."

He gave her a playful shove. "Now I *know* you're not mocking the pizza—not the very bedrock of our skiing society!" He looked so stricken that she burst into laughter again.

"I wouldn't dare," she promised. "Bring on the pizza."

He positioned her on the skis, and they practiced stopping and slowing down and, eventually, "French fries," for when she wanted to speed up, and soon, Beth was no longer terrified by the out-of-control flight down the mountain—she was exhilarated.

Despite all that was unspoken between them, and all the horrible words that had been said and could never be forgotten, things could still be easy between the two of them. She felt she was rediscovering something, or someone, that she hadn't even realized she'd missed. Not Adam—or not just Adam—but herself. The person she had been—before. She thought she'd lost that person forever. Maybe, just maybe, she'd been wrong.

By the time Adam returned, flushed and sunkissed from his day in the snow, Harper was seriously bored—and seriously cranky.

She'd gossiped with Kaia, made small talk with the steady stream of losers who'd returned to the lodge with bumps and bruises of their own, read through this month's *Vogue,* twice—at one point she'd gotten so desperate for something to do that she'd actually called her *mother.* In short: It had been a painfully long afternoon—made even longer by the fact that Adam showed up twenty-three minutes later than he was supposed to. (And yes, she'd been counting.)

But she played the good girlfriend—she put on a happy face.

"How are you doing?" Adam asked, greeting her with a kiss and laying a gentle hand on her wounded ankle.

"Much better, now that you're here," she said truthfully. "So how was your afternoon?"

"Awesome!" he beamed—then looked down at her and quickly corrected himself. "I mean, it was okay. You didn't miss much."

He was so adorable when he tried—and failed—to be a smooth operator.

"It's okay, Ad, I want you to have fun," she assured him. It sounded like the right thing to say . . . even if it wasn't quite true. "So you didn't get too bored, skiing all by yourself? Or did you hook up with one of the guys?"

"No . . ." He stepped behind her, beginning to rub her shoulders. "Actually, I spent most of the day . . ."

His voice trailed off, and Harper tipped her head up to catch a glimpse of his face. What was he thinking?

"Spent most of the day doing what?" she prodded him.

"You know, skiing, just enjoying the outdoors," he said quickly. Too quickly? "But I missed you—how's your knee?"

"It's a little better," Harper said, easing herself up off the couch and balancing on her good leg. "I think if I can lean on you, I should be able to . . . make it back to your room." She hadn't intended for her voice to rise at the end of the sentence, as if it were a question—but then, she didn't know what to expect. Not after last night.

"You can always lean on me, Gracie," he teased, hurrying to her side and slinging an arm around her waist. "Let's just take this one step at a time."

They hobbled out of the lounge and back toward the rooms. Harper smiled. It was so nice to be cradled in Adam's arms, letting him guide her and support her, that the pain in her knee was almost worth it. Almost.

And then Beth crossed their path—and her smile disappeared.

"Hi, Adam," The Blond One said shyly, ignoring Harper. "You ran off so quickly before . . . when Kane came over . . . well, I just wanted to say thank you for helping me today."

Harper looked sharply over at Adam, whose normally open face was shut up tight. She couldn't read him at all. And she didn't like it.

"And what did this wonderful guy do for you today?" Harper asked, in a sugary sweet tone. She leaned her head against Adam's chest. His heart was pounding.

"He didn't tell you?" Beth's oh-so-innocent smile widened. "He spent his whole afternoon teaching me how to ski. I'm sure you would much rather have been off on the black diamonds or something."

"No, I—" Adam looked down at Harper and cut himself off. He continued in a much more formal, measured tone. "I was happy to help, Beth. Now, we should really get Harper back to the room."

Beth gave Harper a weak smile. It wasn't returned.

"Okay, well—thanks again," she said, offering Adam an awkward little wave. "It was . . . good to catch up."

"Yeah." Adam tugged Harper away, and they began

shuffling down the hall as fast as Harper could hobble.

"That was very sweet of you," Harper said carefully, anger and fear simmering in her chest.

"I didn't plan it—," he began.

"Oh, of course not."

"But you should have seen her out there." He chuckled at the memory. "She had no idea what she was doing."

And that was your problem how?

But Harper stopped herself before the words could pop out of her mouth. She had a choice. She could follow her territorial instincts and make sure Adam knew just how wrong he'd been to spend the day with the enemy. And then *lie* about it. She could pick a fight with him that would probably end up with her limping back to her room, alone. She could leave him secure in the knowledge that she was a jealous, unforgiving harpy—and leave him free to chase after the sweet and innocent princess of his dreams. *What would Beth do?* she wondered. It was galling to even ask herself the question—but, given the starry look in Adam's eyes every time that blond hair crossed his field of vision, maybe it was also her smartest move.

Beth, the doormat, the good girl would likely just bite her tongue. Smile. Tell Adam she was happy to see him move on from his anger. Beth wouldn't care if Adam befriended an old girlfriend—or if she did, she'd know it wasn't her place to say anything. It was the kind of behavior that made Beth into such a limp dishrag, at least in Harper's estimation, but it was also the kind of behavior that made Adam love her. And if that's really what he wanted, maybe it was worth a try.

"Well, she's lucky she had you around to help her,"

Harper said finally, with as much sincerity as she could muster.

"You mean that?" Adam asked, giving her a searching look. "I thought you'd be mad. That's, uh, why I didn't say anything before."

"Of course I'm not mad, Ad—you can hang out with whoever you want. And"—she paused, choking the words out was actually inflicting physical pain—"I'm really glad to see you and Beth getting along better. I'm really happy for you."

Adam pulled her closer to him and kissed the top of her head. "Do you know how amazing you are?" he asked.

Great. Just one problem, Harper thought sourly, beaming up at him. *That wasn't me.*

chapter

6

Kaia pulled her car into the lot of the Lost and Found and switched off the ignition, slamming a fist into the steering wheel. It had been hours since Harper's phone call, but she was just as angry.

He'd wanted her to pity him, stuck in the mountains with a bunch of high schoolers.

"I'd so much rather be with you," he'd sworn.

Right. Me—or the first blonde who crosses his path. Same difference.

Kaia didn't even know *why* she was so angry. It's not like she and Jack Powell were "going steady" or something pathetically absurd like that. You couldn't cheat on someone if you weren't in a relationship, right? Yes, he'd forbidden her to see other guys, and she'd accepted it, for the sake of keeping their secret. He was right: High school boys *did* get jealous—and, eventually, curious. But, she now realized, *he'd* never promised not to see other women. And she had never thought to ask.

And why would she? Wasn't that their thing? No obligations, no attachments, no messy emotions screwing things up and getting in the way.

So she had no right to be mad, no right to be jealous. And if her ego had taken a hit, realizing that, apparently, she wasn't enough for him—well, her ego was pretty tough. It would survive.

And meanwhile . . .

She picked up the flyer she'd tossed on the passenger seat: BLIND MONKEYS! ONE NIGHT ONLY AT THE LOST AND FOUND!

Reed was the lead singer, and had told her about the concert—and though she'd tried her best to forget about it, to forget about *him*, here she was. Their date—or whatever it had been—made less and less sense, the more she thought about it. And for the past twenty-four hours, she'd thought about little else.

Still, she'd promised herself she wouldn't pursue anything. For one thing, he was way beneath her. For another, she had Powell—or at least she would, when he finally returned to town. Besides: garage bands, dive bars, and Kaia didn't mix.

But tonight, after Harper's call, she'd suddenly changed her tune.

Not that she had a sudden craving for smoky air and off-key covers. And she certainly wasn't willing to admit that the thought of Powell with another girl—another woman—had driven her so crazy with jealousy that she'd hopped in the car and driven to this dead-end pit of a bar to throw herself at a pizza boy-cum-tow truck driver-cum high school dropout to be.

So what the hell am I doing here? she thought irritably. *I should just turn around and go.* Now.

But, instead, she opened the door, got out of the BMW, and headed toward the bar.

She didn't know why she was there, or what she was getting herself into—but there was only one way to find out.

Maybe she was just a glutton for punishment.

After a long, hard, and too often painful day of skiing, Miranda was safely back in her room. She could plop down on the bed, pull out her iPod, let some good music wash her tension away. . . . But, instead, she pulled out her computer. She no longer had any delusions that anything good could come from matchmadeinhaven.com—and yet she couldn't squelch that last ounce of hope. She just couldn't stop herself. So she logged on.

Congratulations, **Spitfire**, the following 1 user has expressed interest in your profile. Click here to learn more!

She was sure this latest candidate would be just as much of a loser as the rest, but there was no harm in finding out—just for the sake of curiosity, of course.

User Profile: ReadItAndWeep
Sex: male
Age: 17
Height: 5'9"
Favorite color: the desert sky, just after sunrise
Favorite food: chocolate chip cookies
If I were an animal, I'd be: a lab rat—plenty of

nervous energy and nowhere to go. Just like your typical Grace teenager.

Celebrity I most look like: Brad Pitt

Best lie I've ever told: I look a lot like Brad Pitt.

Three things I can't live without: 1—Woody Allen movies, 2—my copy of *The Fountainhead,* 3—someone to talk to

I am . . . counting down the days of high school like a prisoner waiting for parole. Sick of everyone telling me, "You're such a great guy, why aren't you dating anyone?" And a little embarrassed to be on this website.

You are . . . smart, funny, ambitious, and love to laugh. You hate dating for the sake of dating and are looking for something real. Good-hearted, loyal, and not afraid of a challenge.

It seemed too good to be true. A smart, funny, sensitive guy? Looking for love? And drawn to *Miranda*? She allowed herself a small smile. Maybe there was hope for her yet.

"Oh, that feels *so* good," Kane moaned. He leaned his head back against the rim of the hot tub and closed his eyes. "I could stay here forever."

"Mmm, I know what you mean." Beth stretched out along her side, reveling in the jets of hot water pummeling her sore muscles. Her face tingled in the cold night air.

It was an almost perfect end to an almost perfect day.

Kane hadn't asked anything about her afternoon, and she wasn't about to volunteer the fact that she'd spent the whole time with Adam, skiing and laughing. It had felt almost like old times, the two of them together, anticipating each other's every move, the easy ebb and flow of conversation. As if he'd let himself forget everything that had happened—at least until the end of the day, when they'd parted. They had stayed on safe topics all afternoon, meaningless chatter about the snow, about college applications—but in the end, it had seemed as if he was finally about to say something that mattered. And then he'd spotted Kane in the distance—and his whole face had frozen. And that was it. He'd waved a brusque good-bye, and skied away. As if the whole day had never happened. They were right back where they'd started.

But it's a beginning, Beth thought hopefully. *And maybe now we can . . .*

She cut herself off. Can what? Get back together? It's not like she was still in love with him, or even wanted him back. *Friendship,* she assured herself. That's all she wanted. To reach a point where they wouldn't have to ignore each other in the halls. To know something about what was going on in his life. To have him care what was going on in hers.

That was it—nothing more.

She was with Kane now, exactly where she wanted to be.

He floated lazily across the hot tub to join her and playfully flicked some of the churning water in her face.

She giggled, but before she could splash him back, he grabbed her hands and kissed her.

"You look pretty spectacular in a bikini," he commented when they broke for air, giving her an appreciative glance. "Anyone ever told you that?"

Beth blushed and sank a bit deeper into the water, suddenly very aware of how much of her was exposed.

When she didn't reply, he grinned and flexed a bicep. "Traditionally, now's the time when you tell me how handsome and sexy I look," he pointed out.

Now she splashed him. "Yes, you're a total hottie, babe," she gushed in her best Barbie voice.

He leaned back and closed his eyes again, his face plastered with a smug smile. "Mock me all you want, but you know you wish I was wearing a Speedo."

Beth laughed and nestled herself against him, relaxing into the delicious warmth of the water, the brittle sting of the winter air, the solid body beside her. She suddenly felt very tired—and very content.

So tired and so content that she let her guard down for a moment—and the question she'd been holding in for so long just slipped out.

"Kane?"

"Mmm?"

"Why are you with me?"

He began idly rubbing his hand up and down her arm. "I thought we just established that," he said lightly, without opening his eyes. "You're one hot babe, I'm one hot babe—makes perfect sense to me."

"Seriously, Kane—we've got nothing in common."

"We both like hot tubs," he pointed out. "And bikinis . . ."

She rolled her eyes.

"Come on," she said, exasperated. "I mean it. We're totally different. And I'm nothing like any of the girls you dated before."

He opened his eyes then, and sat up and took her hand. "Have I ever made you think that's a bad thing?" he asked gently.

"No, I just—"

"You're right. You're nothing like them, Beth. And *that's* why I'm with you."

"I just think people must look at us and wonder." Beth sighed. "We don't seem to make any sense." She didn't know why she was saying all these things, not now, but it was as if once she'd started, she couldn't stop herself.

"We make sense to *me*," he insisted. "Who cares what other people think? They don't know us—they don't know me."

Beth touched her hand to his cheek. "Sometimes . . ." she paused—but she'd come so far already, why stop? "Sometimes, I feel like *I* don't know you."

She could feel him tense beneath her fingers, and he shifted away.

"You know me," he countered. "This is me—what you see is what you get. I'm easy."

Beth shook her head. "That's got to be the biggest lie you've ever told me. Easy?" She smiled fondly. "Not so much."

"What do you want from me?" he asked petulantly.

Beth draped an arm around him, wishing he hadn't gotten so defensive—she didn't want to fight. She just wanted to talk. They didn't do much of that, she realized.

"I guess I just want—more," she told him honestly. Spending time with Adam today had reminded her of what it was like to *really* know someone—and she wanted that again, somehow. "I really like you, Kane, and I just want more of you—I want to know all of you."

He perked up suddenly. "Something else we have in common," he pointed out. "I want to know all of you, too. Your lips," he kissed her gently. "Your neck." He kissed her again, soft, brief kisses that grazed her chin and ran down the length of her long neck. "Your beautiful—"

"Kane!" she squirmed away. "We're in public!"

"You're right," he replied, gaping at the surroundings as if he'd only just noticed. "What are we doing here? Come on." He stood and extended a hand to her. "Let's go back to my room. We can start this whole getting to know each other thing."

She stood, without his help, and grabbed a towel as she stepped out of the hot tub and onto the steamy patio. "That's not what I mean, and you know it."

"Hey, get your mind out of the gutter. I meant we should go back to my room and talk . . . for a while." He draped another towel around her shoulders and pulled her close to him, rubbing her shivering body to warm her up. "I really like you, too, Beth," he whispered in her ear. "You're not the only one who wants more."

Beth took a deep breath and closed her eyes, resting her head against his dripping chest. Part of her wanted to go with him—*all* of her wanted to go with him, in fact. Why not? He was handsome and charming, his smile made her tremble, they were in this beautiful, romantic resort, and for whatever reason, he wanted to be with her. And, she realized, she wanted to be with him.

So what was the problem? Why did the thought of stepping into his room and closing the door behind her make her heart race and her muscles tense? She knew what he was expecting out of this weekend. She'd known it from the start. So why did the thought make her hyperventilate?

What is wrong *with me?* she thought in frustration. She'd let her fears torpedo her relationship with Adam. Was she going to be alone the rest of her life because of her stupid issues? Kane wasn't Adam—he'd been patient with her so far, but patience wasn't in his nature, she could tell. How long would he wait?

She opened her mouth to tell him, "Yes, let's go back to your room"—but couldn't choke out the words.

"I've got to go back to my room and dry off, take a shower," she said lamely. She gave him a long kiss, then extricated herself from his embrace.

"You can shower in my—"

"I'll come over later, when I'm done," she promised.

And she so wanted it to be the truth.

But she knew herself.

And so she knew better.

It was like a scene out of a movie, and it couldn't have been more perfect. Adam had lit a fire in the fireplace, and the low flames popped and crackled, filling the room with a fresh, woodsy scent and a warm glow. Harper lay on the bed, her swollen knee elevated, sipping a steaming cup of coffee (with some Baileys poured in for good measure). And the pièce de résistance: Adam, stripped down to his boxers, his tan, taut body lit by the glow of the fire, as if bathed in a golden aura. He was fiddling with the radio, searching for a suitably romantic station—but Harper, tired of waiting, waved him back into bed. A crackling Dixie Chicks song on the local country-western station would just have to do.

As Adam climbed onto the mattress next to her, Harper closed her eyes and was finally able to forget about her throbbing knee, Adam's afternoon with Beth, the horror of the night before—it was all erased by the gentle pressure of his body against hers.

"I've been waiting all day for this." Harper sighed as Adam kissed her, first on the lips, then dotting the skin of her exposed breastbone. "I'm just—ouch!"

"Sorry—your knee?" Adam pulled away hastily but, wincing, Harper rolled over and leaned back into him.

"Forget it. Just—" She kissed his bare chest, rubbing her hands up and down his biceps, his rippled stomach muscles. Everything about him was incredible. "Just relax." She rolled over onto her back and he kissed her again, running his hands through her wild mess of hair. Every inch of her skin was tingling, alive at his touch. She could feel him trembling, and she smiled, knowing that, this time, she could be the teacher and he the student—that she was about to show him things he could never have imagined. His soft breath tickled the side of her neck and she giggled, then caught her breath as, ever so slightly, his lips played their way across her body.

She'd never felt this way, exhilarated, bright with anticipation—not since the first time. Maybe not even then. She'd done it all before, but with Adam, everything was new, everything was—

"Harper?"

"Oh, Adam," she moaned. "You're—"

"Harper?" He pulled away from her and sat up abruptly, his face tense and red. "I . . . can't. I'm sorry, it's—"

"Again?" she asked in disbelief, before she could stop

the word from slipping out. She put a hand on his shoulder, but he shrugged it off.

"I want to. I just . . ."

Harper came up behind him and put her arms around him, teasing her fingers through the soft blond hair on his chest.

"It's okay," she assured him. "It's—this happens." Did it? Certainly never to her. Not before. And not twice in a row.

"It's *not* okay," he exploded in frustration, pushing her away. He rose and began to pace around the room. He was so vibrant, glowing with anger and frustration—she wanted him even more. "Goddamnit! This is just so . . . humiliating."

"Adam," Harper began plaintively, unsure what to say. She got out of bed and went to him, grabbed him, forced him to stand still. "Adam, look at me."

But he refused, and when she lightly grabbed his chin and tried to turn his face in her direction, he squirmed away. It was like talking to a petulant little boy who knew he was about to get in trouble and didn't want to face up to what he'd done.

Or, in this case—hadn't done.

"It's not you," he muttered, staring fixedly at the crackling fire.

Right. What else could it be? After last night with those losers from the basketball team . . . and then he'd spent all day with sweet, virginal Beth. Harper held her breath for a moment, trying to get her emotions under control. Adam was with *her* now—he wanted her. This was all just a fluke. Bad luck, bad timing. It had to be. And they'd get through it.

"Adam, do you want to try—"

"Maybe you should just go," he interrupted her in a rough, husky voice. "It's late, and—"

"Sure. Yeah." Harper backed away from him and hastily began pulling on her clothes. She'd hoped they would at least sleep there together, curled up in each other's arms. Awkward as it was, it was better than . . . nothing.

Don't make a big deal out of it, she instructed herself, *and maybe it doesn't have to be a big deal.*

"We have to get up early tomorrow, anyway, to drive back and"—she faked a yawn—"I'm really tired." She slipped into her heavy coat and zipped it up. Even though she wouldn't actually have to step outside to get back to her room, she was suddenly cold, and wanted something warm and heavy wrapped around her.

"Harper, I—" Adam paused, and finally turned to face her. Standing there in the middle of the room, still half naked, he looked so vulnerable, Harper just wanted to rush to him and assure him everything would be all right. And make him assure her that it didn't mean anything, that he wanted to be with her, as much as ever.

"I guess I'll see you tomorrow," she said instead, affecting a cheerful voice.

"Tomorrow," he agreed. He gave her a lame little wave and took a step toward her, then stopped. "Good night."

Harper forced herself to smile, then limped out the door. None of it meant anything, she assured herself. Sex, no sex, whatever. Adam was falling in love with her, and it didn't matter what his friends said, or how much his pretty princess ex-girlfriend wanted him back—Adam was hers, for good.

She wasn't worried. Of course not. If there was one thing Harper was sure of, it was the power she had over men.

All men. Hadn't she proven that by snagging Adam in the first place? So whatever was going on in Adam's head, it was minor. It was temporary.

It had to be.

Miranda was already in bed and nearly asleep when she heard the door open and saw Harper's shadowy figure tiptoe across the room.

"Wasn't expecting to see you tonight," Miranda said, flipping on the lamp by her bed.

Startled, Harper nearly tripped over herself.

"Let's just say Adam and I wore each other out," she said, giving Miranda a meaningful grin as she began changing into her pajamas.

Miranda laughed—there was nothing she loved more than Harper's post-date epics, although since she'd started dating Adam, the juicy stories had been few and far between.

"So? Spill," Miranda pressed. "Was it worth the wait?"

Harper blushed, and Miranda almost choked. She'd seen Harper's face turn red after a few too many hours in the sun—or a few too many margaritas—but never out of embarrassment. And *never* about a guy.

"A lady doesn't kiss and tell," Harper protested, climbing into bed and tucking herself beneath the garish flowered comforter.

"And that applies to you how?" Miranda asked, ducking as Harper tossed a pillow at her head. "Come on, was it everything you expected?"

"And more," Harper allowed, a secretive smile playing across her lips. "It is *Adam,* after all."

"That's all you're going to tell me?" Miranda shrieked, throwing the pillow back at her best friend.

Harper just laughed. "Come on, Rand, I'm tired. Can we just say it was amazing and incredible, and leave it at that? Dirty details in the morning, I promise."

"Yeah, yeah, fine," Miranda agreed grudgingly. "It's not like I'm living vicariously through you or anything."

"Speaking of which," Harper asked, turning to face Miranda and propping herself up on her elbow, "what did you do tonight? I figured you'd still be out partying."

Decision time. Miranda could admit to Harper, her best friend, who knew everything about her down to the name of her third-grade imaginary friend, what she'd done with her night. That is—nothing. Or, more specifically, nothing, followed by an hour of trolling for dates on the Internet, followed by more nothing. She could confess everything about matchmadeinhaven.com and spend the next two hours sitting up and speculating about the charming and mysterious ReadItAndWeep, and plotting out her next move.

And for a second, it seemed like a fabulous idea. Miranda opened her mouth to spill all—and then caught herself, just in time. Because there was Harper, exhausted from a night of wild, passionate—whatever—with the love of her life. And all Miranda had to offer was an empty bag of Oreos and a new crush on a cybergeek? She could already see the look of patronizing encouragement—or worse, ridicule—that was sure to follow her confession.

No, thank you. Not tonight. She was too tired—and, to

be honest, too secretly excited about ReadItAndWeep—to bear the humiliation. Besides, what were a few more secrets between friends?

"Big party in some kid's room," Miranda said truthfully, avoiding the small fact that she hadn't bothered to attend. "You're right, though, it's late. I'll tell you all about it in the morning." She quickly flipped off her light so that Harper couldn't read the lie on her face. A moment later, the light over Harper's bed went out, too, casting them both in darkness.

"Miranda?" Harper suddenly asked, her disembodied voice sounding strangely hesitant.

"Yes?"

There was a long pause, then—

"Nothing. I'm just . . . glad you had such a great night." Miranda sighed. Little did she know.

"Not as great as yours," she chirped. Also true. "You're so lucky to have someone like Adam."

"That's me," Harper said drily. "The luckiest girl in the world."

Reed's band sucked.

Kaia didn't know too much about music—but then, she didn't have to, because whatever the band was playing didn't really qualify.

It was loud, all right, and did seem to somehow involve instruments. But the guitarist's screeching solos sounded like a drowning cat, and the drummer, off in a world of his own, had abandoned any kind of rhythm for the random clanging and pounding you might expect from a three-year-old left alone with a pile of pots and pans. The overall effect was slightly less than melodic.

As for the bar . . . Kaia's short time in Grace had quickly revealed to her that the nightlife options were rather lacking—but this place topped the list of dumps. It was overwhelmingly brown, from the padded imitation leather walls to the bartender's cigarette-stained teeth. A couple of arcade games were tucked into the corner, along with a jukebox and what looked—at least from a safe distance away—like a coin-operated porn viewer. The walls were covered with the tattered remnants of holiday decorations—a year's worth of holidays, from sagging and faded Fourth of July flags to ripped four-leaf clovers. A handful of surly loners nursed their drinks at rickety tables, and a group of burly, middle-aged men, apparent escapees from a Teamsters' convention, roared with drunken laughter by the beer-stained pool table.

If there had been a stack of comment cards, Kaia would have recommended that the management erect a new sign on the fake saloon doors out front: ABANDON HOPE, ALL YE WHO ENTER HERE. It would be both an appropriate sentiment and a public service.

After her first sip of flat beer and the opening chords of the Blind Monkeys' first "song," she'd almost walked out.

And then Reed had begun to sing.

The song was horrible, the original lyrics lamely unoriginal, and the backup band worthless. But Reed's voice . . . it was like barbed wire draped in velvet. Low and hoarse, but warm, and with an intensity that scared her—and drew her in. He leaned in toward the mike and gazed out at the audience, and his eyes seemed to meet hers, then flicker past. Kaia couldn't look away.

He wore a tight-fitting navy T-shirt and black jeans, and his face was framed by a tangled halo of jet-black curls that kept flopping down over his eyes.

He'd clean up nicely, she mused—but the idea of Reed Sawyer in a Hugo Boss suit and Bruno Magli loafers seemed laughable, and wrong. His look fit him—just as the bar fit him, the town fit him. She was repelled by all of it—so why couldn't she tear herself away?

The band played for an hour, driving most of the regulars out of the bar in search of a quieter hole in which to hide. But Kaia stayed. When the set finally ended, Reed stepped off stage, obviously exhausted. She knew he had seen her—but he didn't smile, didn't wave, didn't come over. Instead, he walked slowly to the bar, where the bartender—an overweight brunette in a low-cut top—had a drink waiting for him. He sat down on a stool with his back to Kaia.

No one turned his back on Kaia.

And she wasn't about to go up to him. She didn't even want to, not really—what would be the point?

So, instead, she sat there for a few minutes, sipping some water and refusing to look in his direction. Then she made a decision: enough. She got up from her seat, grimacing as her heel sank into something suspiciously soft and moist on the sticky floor, and walked out of the bar.

The parking lot was shadowy and half empty—and when she got to her car, there was a dark figure leaning against it. Her heart leaped into her throat—and then she recognized his silhouette. It was Reed.

"Where did you——?"

"There's a back exit," he explained, jerking his head toward the bar. "I saw you go. Leaving without saying good-bye?"

"Without saying *hello*," Kaia corrected him. "But it's unfortunately too late for that." He somehow brought out the nasty in her, just by breathing. And he just stood there and took it—almost as if he knew her, could recognize the feeble attempt to drive him away. Maybe she was glad it hadn't worked.

"Did you like the show?"

"It . . . had its moments."

"Yeah, we suck," he acknowledged. "I didn't expect to see you here."

"I'm not very predictable," Kaia said, taking a step toward him. In the dim orange glow of the flickering streetlight, she could barely make out his features, and his eyes were only pools of darkness—unreadable. "I'm rarely what you'd expect."

"I know," he told her, and took a step closer as well.

They were almost touching, and she could feel a shiver of electricity pass between them, as if the air itself were charged with tension. Possibility.

"I should get back inside," he said, but didn't move.

"I should get home," she agreed, but she, too, kept still.

"I wish it would rain again," she said suddenly, nonsensically. And it was true.

"It will," he promised. And he took one more step and the space between them disappeared. Her lips met his hungrily and she sucked in the taste of him, sweet and sharp at the same time. She thrust herself against him and pushed him against the side of the car, drinking in the feel of his hands roaming across her body.

He pulled away first, her skin still craving his touch.

"I'm going now," he said simply, with the mocking smile she loved to hate. "I'll see you around."

And he was gone.

chapter

7

It's tough to have a bad time when you're nestled amid the ice-covered peaks with nothing to do but frolic in the snow and bring your wildest romantic fantasies to life. Opportunity is everywhere. You have to really work to avoid it.

They'd managed.

A waste, Adam thought as he unpacked his duffel bag and came across the unused pack of condoms. *A total, fucking waste.* He threw them across the room toward the wastebasket. Missed.

A disaster, Harper thought, pressed up against her window, watching Adam's bedroom window a few yards away. All those hopes and all those expectations—and they'd all come to nothing. He turned out the light and then, almost as an afterthought, pulled down the shade. Almost as if he knew she was watching.

A mess, Beth thought, as Kane dropped her off at home and, with barely a peck good-bye, sped away into the night.

The trip had started out so well—and then it had just fallen apart. Why did she always make everything so complicated? Why couldn't it just be simple, for once? Easy. Straightforward. Clean.

A miscalculation, Kane thought, speeding down the dark, empty highway. He'd pushed too hard, been too obvious. Not a problem. He could do slow. He could do subtle. He could do whatever was needed to get the job done.

A mistake, Kaia thought, lying in bed and wondering whether Powell was home yet, when he would call. That's all it had been. All *he* had been. A terrible mistake. A moment of weakness. She'd indulged temptation, no harm done. But it was back to reality now. Reed Sawyer was nothing but a mistake—one that could never happen again.

Although one in ten men suffer from impotence at some point in their lives, the disorder remains largely misunderstood, due to the persistent shroud of embarrassment and shame that accompanies the condition.

You can say that again, Adam thought bitterly. It had taken him a full hour to even work up the nerve to type "impotence" into his computer's search engine—and as he read through the numerous and mostly unhelpful Web sites, he couldn't stop looking over his shoulder every ten seconds, even though he knew there was no one home to catch him.

Impotency can be attributed to psychological or physical causes. But fear not! Whatever the root of your condition, there are answers, if you're willing to look for them. There's no need to suffer in silence any longer!

Condition. It was such a harsh, clinical term. But then, most of the Web sites Adam had managed to find were exactly that: harsh. Clinical. And thoroughly depressing. Somehow, reading about surgical procedures and hydraulic penile implants was not improving his mood.

This wasn't for him. He wasn't some graying, middle-aged guy who needed a fistful of Viagra to get it up—he was a healthy, athletic, eighteen-year-old guy in his sexual prime. Tomorrow night was the first basketball game of the season, and everyone watching him sprint across the court would assume he was just as strong and virile as he looked—young, fit, with all his parts in working order. They'd never guess what was really going on—and, while he was on the subject, what the hell *was* going on?

Psychological causes can include stress, guilt, depression, and relationship problems.

Adam sighed, and pushed himself away from the computer. So he was messed up—like that was a surprise. A month ago, he'd been happy, relaxed, confident—then Beth and Kane had bashed the hell out of him, and now he didn't know who he was or what he could rely on.

The worst part was, in the past, Adam might have been able to swallow his pride and gone to Kane for help on this one. But now, he had no one to ask—no older brother, no trusted friend, and he hadn't talked to his father in years. And the Web was obviously useless.

No, he was on his own. There wasn't much he could do about his stress level, but he could at least reassure himself that the cause wasn't physical. He pulled an old *Playboy* out from beneath his mattress. It couldn't hurt to remind his body of what it was supposed to do.

After all—practice makes perfect.

"Yo, Gracie, this slaw isn't going to clean itself up!"

Harper winced. It was one thing when Adam called her "Gracie"—hearing the nickname in his lilting Southern accent reminded her of all those lazy summer afternoons they'd spent chasing each other around the backyard during childhood. Calling Harper "Gracie" had been the surest way for Adam to end the afternoon flat on his back with a wad of dirt stuffed in his mouth. (Though, even then, Harper had secretly loved it.) But when Mr. White, the diner manager, adopted his little pet name for her, it made her skin crawl—and it usually meant she had a particularly disgusting task awaiting her.

There was one week left of winter break, and Harper had planned to spend every spare minute at the diner, in hopes she could pay back her parents and quit by New Year's. It had seemed like a good idea in theory—but, in practice, it sucked. Especially today. *Merry Christmas to me,* she thought bitterly. *Ho, ho, ho.*

The laughter was appropriate—her life was a joke.

"And when you're done in there, Gracie, come back

here and see me. I've got a little holiday treat for you."

"Yes, Mr. White," she called out as sweetly as she could, still determined to demonstrate that she could be a model employee even under the most heinous of circumstances.

White had promised to try her out on table service today, since she was the only waitress forced to be there. But surprise, surprise, there were no customers. And so Harper was stuck spending Christmas with her new best friends, Mr. Mop and Mr. Bucket.

All this so she could pay her parents back for the ski trip? *WFS.* Right. She and Adam were supposed to be closer than ever by now—instead? They'd barely seen each other since getting back. Harper had, of course, been stuck at the diner. And she suspected that Adam was hiding out.

"Any day now, Gracie!"

Harper sighed and slogged toward White's "office," expecting to find him, as usual, with his feet kicked up on the desk, watching TV and picking his nose.

"Yes, Mr. White?" she said, affecting a subservient tone—it didn't come easy—and poking her head in. "What did you—ew!" Harper stopped short in the doorway. There was White. Way too much of him. As she'd expected, he was leaned back in his chair, his tree-trunk legs propped up on the desk, and the local public-access Christmas show blaring in the background. Just one problem. He was wearing a half-unbuttoned, cream-colored (or at least it looked like it used to be cream colored) shirt with sweat stains rimming his pits and a forest of chest hair poking through—and barely anything else. His thick, hairy legs were totally bare.

"What's your problem?" Mr. White growled.

"I—I—" Harper wasn't struck speechless very often, but then, how often was one trapped in a dingy back room with your hairy half-naked boss?

Still, she had an image to protect.

"What did you want, Mr. White?" she asked, maintaining a neutral tone. "I'm kind of busy out there."

"Just thought I'd give you your Christmas treat," White said, standing up.

A Christmas bonus? Dare she hope?

"You don't mind the *ensemble,* do you?" he asked with a sly grin that said he knew exactly how much she minded and was loving every minute of it. "I figured, since it was just the two of us . . ."

He approached her, shirt flapping against his bare legs, and Harper forced herself to stand her ground. *Is he really stupid enough to try something?* she wondered, swiftly calculating her options. He was big, yes—but also fat, slow, and stupid. She'd kick him in the balls, she decided, and then sue him for everything he had. This whole sordid episode could turn out to be a blessing in disguise.

"You see, round this time of year, I like to do a little something extra for my *special* employees," White explained, leering at her. "And you're one of my special employees, Gracie, aren't you?"

Steady, Harper prepared herself. *Wait for your moment.*

He lumbered toward her.

Closer, closer—

And then he was past her—bending down to get something in the corner. Harper watched in confusion. If she wasn't getting a bonus, and she wasn't getting sexually harassed, what the hell was she doing there?

"Here ya go!" White said triumphantly, standing up and tossing her a huge cloth sack. "Merry Christmas! Ho, ho, ho!"

"And this would be?" Harper wrinkled her nose and carefully set the bag on the ground. It smelled even worse than she did, and after a full day of mopping up the diner's bathrooms, that was saying a lot.

"It's laundry day, sweetie. As you can see—" He gestured toward his lower half. "I'm fresh outta pants. And—" here he leaned toward her and winked. "I'm *almost* out of unmentionables. If you know what I mean."

Harper recoiled from his hot, musty breath—and left the bag on the ground.

"I'll give you ten bucks to take care of this today. And if you do a good job, you can do it every week." He turned away from her and sat down at his desk again. "You're welcome."

"You want *me* to . . . do your laundry?" Harper could feel her good employee routine slipping through her fingers. "Are you kidding me?"

"Don't play coy with me, sweetie," White said, gazing at the TV. "You may have a fancy name, but I know you need the cash." He chuckled. His laugh sounded like a garbage disposal. "Otherwise, why the hell would you be working here?"

Harper looked down at her feet. She could see a dirty gray piece of cotton peeking out of the top of the bag, but didn't want to think too hard about what it might be.

As she saw it, she had two options.

She could suck it up and take the laundry, prove to herself and the world that, contrary to popular opinion, Harper Grace didn't mind a little hard work once in a while. More importantly, she could pay back her parents that much faster, hastening the blessed day when she could finally walk out of the Nifty Fifties and never come back.

Or she could throw the bag of dirty underwear in his face and remind this loser that class and money were two separate things. He may have her beat on the latter, but where the former was concerned, he wasn't even worthy enough to shine her shoes.

"Oh, what, did I offend you?" he snarled. "*Bethie* never had a problem with it."

Harper rolled her eyes. Of course not. Little Miss Perfect let White walk all over her. Watching Beth get bawled out by the manager on a daily basis had been the only glimmer of pleasure in Harper's dark diner days.

What would Beth do?

Beth would probably accept the laundry gratefully, like a dog begging for scraps. *Beth* would smile sweetly and thank White for his Christmas "bonus." *Beth* would hold her nose, wash the underwear, and come back eager for more torture.

But Harper wasn't Beth—thank God. And it was about time people started to appreciate it.

She gave the bag of laundry a sharp kick, pretending her foot was connecting with something far more satisfying. It skidded across the room, strewing pants and underwear all over the office floor.

"Did you forget who you're dealing with here?" White growled, standing up. His face had turned a deep, purplish red.

"No—I forgot who *you* were dealing with," Harper

corrected him. "But now I remember. And just in time."

"What's that supposed to mean?"

"It means I used to think your burgers were the nasti-est thing in town—and then I met you. I quit."

Kaia was having a bad day. And the e-mail didn't help.

```
K—Merry X-Mas! New Year's at Smash.
Be there!—L P.S. J's been asking
about you. . . .
```

Lauren was the only one of her New York "friends" who kept in touch with regular—if brief—e-mails, tantalizing missives about the life Kaia had left behind. She was also the only one who didn't rub Kaia's face in the fact that she was missing everything. And "J" was, of course, Joshua Selznick, an ex-boyfriend with a model's build and a mogul's wallet.

Kaia fantasized for a moment about making a grand re-entry to New York for New Year's Eve. A private party at Smash, one of the hottest clubs in the city (and, conve-niently, owned by a friend's father). A wild, all-night adven-ture filled with glitz and glamour, just like the old days . . .

New Year's had always been Kaia's favorite day of the year, but her father had all the power—and all the credit cards. Which meant she was stuck.

Unless . . .

Kaia was pretty sure her mother hated her, but there was one person she hated more: Kaia's father. Motherly affection might not be enough to win her approval for a trip back east—but maybe divorcée disgust would.

Such a strategy would, of course, mean contacting her

mother—but sometimes it was necessary to make a small sacrifice for the greater good. Five minutes later, she was dialing the number, half hoping there would be no answer.

"What is it?" came the harsh greeting.

"Mother?" Kaia asked tentatively.

"Oh, darling, it's you. I thought it was your *father*. Caller ID, you know. What is it, darling? I'm running out."

Kaia always marveled at the way her mother was able to take a word of apparent affection, like "darling," and somehow drain it of all warmth.

"It's been a while since we've talked," Kaia began.

"Oh, has it?" her mother asked distractedly.

"Four months, Mother," she pointed out.

"Oh no, I'm sure it hasn't been that long. Don't be melo-dramatic, darling. Well, it was nice to hear from you, but—"

"It's Christmas, Mother. Don't you even want to know how I am?" Kaia asked through gritted teeth.

"You sound lovely, darling. I assume your father's tak-ing proper care of you."

"That's the thing—"

"I can only hope he's managing to be a better father than he was a husband. That bottom-feeding, scum-sucking . . . well, it's all in the past now. You're an angel for putting up with him."

"He's not around very much," Kaia admitted.

"Oh, then lucky you!" her mother exclaimed. "Now Kaia, I really must go, so—"

"I want to come home for a visit," Kaia blurted out. "Dad won't let me—he's trying to keep me away from you. I—" Could she really get the words out with a straight face? "I miss you."

"Oh. Well, that won't do at all," Kaia's mother said calmly. "Who does your father think he is? Of course we'll plan a visit. Sometime soon, darling. Don't worry."

"I was thinking next weekend," Kaia said, hope rising.

Her mother laughed, a brittle, glassy trill that contained no real amusement or joy. "The weekend? Oh no, I'm far too busy. It's New Year's, you know."

She knew.

"And, of course, the rest of winter is just a mess—so many benefits to attend, you know how it is. But don't worry, we'll find some time—maybe in the spring. Or definitely in the summer."

"I'm moving back in the summer," Kaia pointed out coolly.

"Of course, of course—well, that's perfect, then. It's been lovely hearing from you, darling."

"But—"

"Let's chat again soon, shall we?"

And the line went dead.

Once upon a time, there was a shy young girl who wanted nothing more than to get out of her small-town life and see the world. She thought she'd be trapped in her tiny, boring house forever—and then one magical day, she opened a book. And the whole world changed.

Beth crumpled up the paper in disgust. It was so melodramatic, so cheesy—so lame. Almost as bad as her first effort:

My name is Beth Manning and I would love to attend (Your School Here). I am bright and energetic, the editor of my school newspaper, and I think I could make an excellent addition to (Your School Here).

Yeah, that was great. She might as well just submit a blank page with the heading "I am so boring, I have literally nothing to say for myself. Please admit me, anyway."

Out of desperation, she'd checked out *How to Write a Winning College Essay* from the Grace local library—hoping that even though it was written in 1987, it would still help her get over her writer's block. But so far? Nothing.

Be creative, the book urged. *Be yourself.* Unless "yourself" is weird or just totally bland, Beth thought dispiritedly. Then maybe it was best to be someone else.

She wondered if Harper was even bothering to fill out her applications (the way things were going, maybe she'd just steal Beth's). How might her essay read? "I'm Harper Grace, and I'll be attending your school next year, because I want to—and, let's be honest, I always get what I want."

But Beth was too sickened by the thought of Harper to continue down that road—because that led to Harper-and-Adam, and *that* usually led to her leaning over the toilet, waiting for a wave of nausea to pass.

Be honest, the book kept saying. *Talk about what you want, what you're proud of. Why you're special.*

But how was she supposed to do that in an essay when she couldn't do it in real life? She didn't seem to know how to be honest about what she wanted anymore—not with Kane, not with Adam, not with herself. And she had no idea who she was anymore. Before, it had been easy. Beth, the good girl. Everyone knew it. But now? She smiled, thinking of how much she'd enjoyed tormenting Harper at the diner, how she'd managed to convince Mr. White to saddle her with the dreaded Christmas shift. Was that the work of a good girl?

Maybe honesty was the answer after all.

I used to be the perfect student, the perfect daughter, the perfect girlfriend. Then my boyfriend dumped me, I tanked the SATs—and now I don't know who I am or what I'm doing. I do know that I still want a future, and I want it away from here—and that if you take a chance on me, it just might pay off.

Well . . . it was a start.

Just not a good one.

Mercifully, the phone rang, and although Beth had promised herself no breaks until she'd finished a draft, she leaped to answer it.

"Hey, it's me—what are you doing?"

Beth wondered—was it strange that she'd been dating Kane for over a month and a part of her still found it a little bizarre that he was a part of her life, that they spoke so often that she was expected to recognize his voice? She did, of course—but something about the casual intimacy still threw her off. She just wished she knew why. "Working." She sighed. "Sort of."

"It's Christmas," he pointed out.

"Don't remind me. My brothers are on a massive sugar

high from all the candy canes. From the sound of it, they're having some kind of shouting contest."

"I know, I can hear it."

"What? Where—" Beth went over to her window and looked out. Sure enough, Kane was lounging against a tree. He smirked at the sight of her and gave her a languid wave. "What are you doing out there?" she asked, laughing. "Do you want to come in?"

"Actually . . ." And in that pause, Beth was reminded of how much Kane hated her house. He'd never said anything, of course, but whenever he stepped inside, she could tell it got to him—the noise, the clutter, the size (or lack thereof). It didn't usually bother her, but when Kane was there, it felt like a zoo—she was just glad he didn't think of her as one of the animals.

"I was hoping you could come out and play," he said, affecting an innocent little-boy voice.

Beth giggled.

"I've got all this stuff to do, my essay—"

"Just for a little break? I'm booooored," he whined.

"Well . . . I do have to give you your Christmas present," she mused. "And maybe if it were just a quick break."

"You can't resist me," Kane boasted and, giving her another wave, snapped his phone shut. Beth shook her head. For whatever reason, it was true.

Victory. He'd gotten her away from her work and out of the house—but was it normal that those be such major triumphs? Never having had a real girlfriend before, Kane didn't really have any idea how often you were supposed to see her or what you were supposed to do when you did—and with Adam still pouting, he didn't have anyone to ask.

While he hadn't gotten everything—or really, anything—he'd wanted out of Beth up in the mountains, Kane was no quitter, not when it came to beautiful women. And then there was the disconcerting fact that he was actually enjoying her company—fully clothed, out of bed, inches of space between them, and he still wanted her around. It didn't make any sense.

Not that there weren't a few occasional perks.

"Mmm," he breathed when they broke from a long kiss hello. "You smell amazing. What is that?"

"Um." She blushed and tucked her hair behind her ears—a nervous habit that, Kane was ashamed to admit, he was beginning to find adorable. "Shampoo?"

"So what's this I hear about a present?" he asked, taking her hand and leading her down the sidewalk.

She gave him a playful shove. "You're such a little kid sometimes—can't you wait?"

"I'm nothing if not patient," he pointed out, only half joking. After all, she had no idea how long he'd waited around for her. Was still waiting.

"It's just something little," she said hesitantly, pulling a small wrapped box from her coat pocket. "I hope you like it."

"You've got nothing to worry about, babe," he said, slinging an arm around her. "I'll love it."

He unwrapped the gift. Inside the box lay a CD case, with a picture of the two of them together taped to the cover.

Total cheese.

"I . . . I put together some songs I thought you'd like," she explained. "You know, music that made me think of you."

"Oh, Beth." He slipped the CD into his pocket and gave her a kiss. It was so hokey, so painfully sincere, so . . . Beth. "I love it." And it wasn't a *total* lie. "I can't wait to get home and listen to it." Except for that part. Kane shuddered to think what kind of lovey-dovey crap Beth might have burned for him.

"Your present isn't quite ready yet," Kane explained, though the truth was, he'd forgotten. It had been a long time since he'd needed to buy someone a Christmas present.

"Kane, you don't need to get me anything else," she complained, fondling the blue cashmere tucked around her neck. "This scarf is so beautiful, and so expensive—"

He cut her off with a kiss. "Your gift is coming," he said firmly, "and you'll love it." Whatever it turned out to be. "So, what are you up to for the rest of the day?"

"Kane, it's Christmas. I've got all this family stuff."

"Of course you do," he said heartily. "I knew that." Though, actually, the idea hadn't occurred to him. Family. Another stupid tradition he'd forgotten. Along with Christmas lights and presents.

"What about you? Are you and your father . . . ? Or do you want to come home with me?"

"No," he said hastily. "I've got family stuff of my own." If "family stuff" meant beer and cold pizza alone, wondering if his father would remember it was Christmas and actually come home that night.

For a second, Kane was tempted. He hadn't had a

real Christmas, a family Christmas, since his mother died. After that, it had been just him and his brother, getting drunk, laughing at the loser carolers, and then, when Aaron went off to college, it was just him. Beth's Christmas, on the other hand, was probably straight out of a Hallmark commercial: stockings hanging from the mantel, wrapping paper all over the floor, disgusting displays of Christmas spirit. And for a second, Kane was tempted. Why not let Beth play Tiny Tim to his Scrooge, teach him the true meaning of blah, blah, blah.

The fact that he was getting bored just imagining it? Probably not a great sign.

Maybe he was too old for Christmas. Maybe he was just over it.

"Are you sure?" Beth asked dubiously. "Because we'd love to have you. I'd love for you to be there."

Kane sighed. Whenever he was around her, he felt like letting down his guard. It was dangerous—and yet strangely appealing. Like a drug he couldn't stay away from.

"I'm sure," he told her, cupping her chin in his hands and tipping her face up toward his for a farewell kiss. Kane believed in drugs—but he didn't believe in losing control. Which meant it was time to go.

She had known the bar would be open on Christmas. It was just that kind of place. Dingy, graying, scattered with familiar faces, the faithful pilgrims who came in almost every night, looking for—something. They never found it. But they kept coming back.

It was a bar for people who had nowhere else to go—especially on Christmas.

And it was Powell's favorite.

After the pleasant chat with her mother, Kaia had needed to get out of the house. Have some fun. And she'd known just where to go. She hadn't heard from Powell since he'd returned from the ski trip, but she was sure it didn't mean anything. So he'd had a little fun, and a little ski bunny, while he was away. It's a free country. It's not like she hadn't had a little fun of her own. That night with Reed might have been an aberration, a freakish fluke that could never be repeated—but it had definitely been hot.

Playtime was over. And Kaia had no doubt that Powell was just waiting for the perfect moment to summon her. The bunny was—must be—history. After all, you don't trade in caviar for tuna fish, and Kaia was caviar all the way.

Still, Kaia decided, it couldn't hurt to show her face, remind him of what he should have been missing. Besides, it was Christmas, and he deserved a holiday treat. Whoever said "'tis better to give than to receive" had obviously never met Kaia Sellers.

She'd dressed herself in red and green from head to toe: red backless top, green peasant skirt, red kitten heels, and, to top it off, a red velvet ribbon tied around her waist. *Aren't you going to unwrap your present?* She rehearsed the line in her head, loving the way the words sounded, and could already see the look on his face. He'd feign annoyance, of course—she was supposed to wait for him to beckon her, that's what they'd agreed on. Those were the rules. No speaking in public, no dating other guys, no obligations, and, most of all, no surprises.

According to the rules, she should be sitting home, biding her time, waiting for him to call.

But Kaia had never been too good with rules.

She almost walked by the bar—from the outside, it was nothing but a narrow gray cement block, with a small, dark, unmarked door. She swung it open and stood in the doorway, waiting for her eyes to adjust.

He wasn't at his normal stool at the end of the bar, nose buried in a book. Instead, he was tucked into one of the few booths lining the wall. He was sipping a glass of red wine. And he wasn't alone.

The ski bunny, Kaia thought with disgust. It had to be. She was blond, lithe, limber, her face radiating a gentle, trusting imbecility—and she was perched on Powell's lap, nuzzling his neck.

Other girls might have confronted him, or started to cry—or just slunk away into the night. But Kaia was better than that. So she just stood there and watched. Waited.

Until, finally, he noticed her. While the ski bunny gave his ear a tongue massage, Powell's eyes met Kaia's, his expression unreadable. Was that guilt in his eyes? Anger? Dismissal? Fear?

Kaia didn't know—and didn't really care. What Jack Powell felt, what he wanted, was beside the point. She'd let him think he was in charge of their little "relationship"— a nice power trip for him that didn't cost her anything. But that was over now.

Powell liked rules so much? Maybe it was time to give him a new set—show him whose game they were really playing. Kaia gave Powell—who hadn't taken his eyes off her, despite the squirming blonde in his lap—a slow, cruel smile. Then turned around and left the bar.

Calm down, she instructed herself, taking a few deep breaths and forcing the anger away. She couldn't get emotionally involved, not if she was going to win this little battle of the wills.

And she was going to win.

She always did.

chapter

8

The phone rang twice before he picked it up—just enough time for Harper to change her mind, almost hang up, then reconsider once again. She'd been over and over this in her head and had concluded that, humiliating as it was, she just had no other choice.

If she was careful, and lucky, her parents would never find out that she'd quit her job—but she still owed them $300, and there were no job openings anywhere in town. So unless she wanted to sell off all her possessions—or her organs—she was stuck. Trapped. With only one very unappealing escape route.

"Grace—to what do I owe this pleasure?"

Kane. Supercilious, haughty, but loaded. All she needed to do was ask him—

But Harper found she couldn't quite get the words out. Maybe if she did it fast, like a Band-Aid. "I need . . . a . . . favor."

Or painfully slow could work, too.

"I'm listening."

Harper silently cursed her parents for sticking her in this position. If they'd only given her the money for the ski trip in the first place, no strings attached, she wouldn't be stuck groveling like this.

Things could be worse, she reminded herself—she could be abasing herself in front of Kaia. Or worse, Beth. Kane was an ass, and he would probably hold this over her head until graduation, but on the plus side, she didn't really care what he thought of her. After all, it was Kane. She'd helped him steal his best friend's girlfriend—so who was he to judge?

"I need to borrow some money," she said flatly. "Three hundred dollars."

"Whoa," he whistled. "Dare I ask why?"

"No."

"And when will I be getting this loan repaid, with interest?"

Good question.

"I don't know."

Bad answer.

"Now Grace, pray tell, why would I possibly do this for you?"

"Because you've got no reason not to?" Harper suggested, knowing that, for Kane, it was usually as good a reason as any. And certainly more palatable than throwing herself on his mercy. "Because you might find it amusing to have me in your debt?"

"Ah, Grace, you know me so well," he marveled, and Harper breathed a silent sigh of relief. "So when should I deliver this windfall?" Kane asked. "Tonight?"

"Only if you're going to be at the basketball game,"

Harper said, rolling her eyes. "I have to be there to 'support my man.'" Vomit. Beth had always been Adam's eager good luck charm and one-woman cheering section. So Harper was forcing herself to play along—but lame high school sporting events were so not her thing.

"Just save some of that school spirit for me," Kane requested.

"You?"

"Haven't you heard? I'm back, baby. Starting point guard, making my varsity debut."

"You?" Harper repeated.

"What? Can't I lend my many talents to our school's proudest team? Besides, have you seen those cheerleaders?"

"What are you really up to, Kane?"

"What's the money for, Grace?"

"Point taken." She knew it was stupid, but being too poor to pay for the ski trip was just too embarrassing. Better Kane should think she had some dark, nefarious purposes. Keeping up an image was hard work. "So, you can give me a check tonight?"

"I'll be there," Kane promised. "And so will my money. Just one thing, Harper."

"What's that?" she asked, suddenly wary. Kane never called her by her first name.

"This is a lot of money."

"I know, and I'll pay it back when—"

"In the meantime," Kane said, "you owe me."

"I just said, I'll pay you—"

"No, not money," he corrected her. "A favor. Quid pro quo. And when I call it in, you'd better be ready to deliver."

Miranda answered the phone with a weary sigh. "No," she said, before Harper could speak.

"It'll be fun, Rand, I swear."

"Now, where have I heard that before?" But Miranda was smiling. She loved those rare occasions when Harper was forced to beg, and she had to admit, it was good to feel needed again, special . . . but that didn't mean she was giving in. "Like I told you the last time you called, and the time before that, I'm not going. Do you know how boring basketball is?"

"Um, yes," Harper replied in a "duh" voice. "Why do you think I need you to come with me? Besides, you know that's not the real reason you won't go."

"Nice of you to throw that back in my face, Harper," Miranda said in annoyance. She flipped open her computer—waiting for it to emerge from sleep mode so she could check her e-mail. See if *he* had written. "You *know* why I can't go."

"Maybe if you're nice to him, he'll let you try on his costume," Harper suggested, choking back laughter.

Miranda groaned, but had to laugh along. It was funny, when you thought about it, that the only guy who'd been interested in her all year had turned out to be the school mascot, a bumbling loser who hadn't minded dressing up like a big green cactus as the whole school jeered at him.

Although . . . it had been kind of nice, having someone like Greg dote on her for a week or two. And he hadn't been *that* big a loser. At least, not until she'd blown him off and he'd turned into the king of the assholes. Miranda shook her head, trying to knock all thoughts of Greg out of her brain. This was *exactly* why she couldn't go to the game.

Besides, she thought, opening up her e-mail, she had other things on her mind. Better things—better guys.

"Kane will be there," Harper wheedled. "He's on the team now."

Kane Geary, running up and down the court in those tight gym shorts . . .

"I don't care," Miranda lied. "Besides, what happened to your whole 'forget about Kane' mantra?"

The computer *dinged*.

You have new mail.

It was him.

"I know what I said, Rand, but you never know, and—"

"I know you're desperate, Harper, but this is just pathetic," Miranda told her, distractedly scanning the e-mail. ReadItAndWeep was online—and wanted her IM name so they could chat. The e-mail had been sent only a few minutes earlier—would he still be there? Could she risk a live chat? Could she risk missing it? "Look, I've got to go, I have stuff to do."

"What stuff? It's winter break! Come on, for me?"

"Bye, Harper. Have fun at the game!"

"But—"

Miranda hung up on her. It was rude, she knew—but she also knew Harper, and this was the only way to get her to shut up. Besides, she was in a hurry.

Spitfire: Hey, U still there?
ReadItAndWeep: Thought you'd never ask. How goes it?

Spitfire: You live here—how do you think?
ReadItAndWeep: B-O-R-I-N-G
Spitfire: Bingo.

But she was lying—she was far from bored. "Talking" to ReadItAndWeep was, in fact, the highlight of her day. His e-mails had been so witty and articulate—and as they frantically typed back and forth to each other, she was pleased to discover that his real-time persona was even better.

ReadItAndWeep: NEVER seen *Annie Hall*? Unbelievable!
Spitfire: YOU've never seen *Bring It On*.
ReadItAndWeep: Not the same thing.
Spitfire: Right—your movie sucks. Mine = a modern classic.
ReadItAndWeep: You dare to insult the master? Blasphemy! You ready to dodge the lightning bolts?

Miranda laughed out loud. She felt like she could "talk" to him for hours—even if he did worship at the altar of Woody Allen.

Spitfire: I think I'll risk it.
ReadItAndWeep: A risk-taker. I'm impressed. You up for another one?
Spitfire: ???
ReadItAndWeep: I think we should meet. Face-to-face. What do you think?
ReadItAndWeep: Spitfire?

ReadItAndWeep: Hello?
ReadItAndWeep: Anyone out there?

Miranda stared at the keyboard, frozen with fear. She couldn't bring herself to answer.

But she couldn't bring herself to log off.

Kaia winced at the booming, off-key "music" emerging from the marching band, which had just wound its way around the court and was now dispersing its members through the bleachers. The better to deafen the audience, apparently.

It was her first public school sporting event—and it was just as loud, tedious, and tacky as it always looked in the movies. Cheerleaders stumbling all over themselves, crazed fans with their faces painted in the school colors—rust and mud—and down on the court, a bunch of beautiful boys running aimlessly up and down the hardwood floor, getting all hot and bothered about a stupid ball going through a stupid hoop. Pretty to watch—but such a waste of all that sweaty exertion.

So what was she doing there?

It had seemed unlikely enough for Harper to invite her along—even Harper seemed surprised when Kaia actually agreed to go.

But Harper had said those magic words: "Everyone will be there." And, when pushed to clarify, had explained that "everyone" included all the Haven High students—*and* all the teachers. Which meant everyone's favorite British bachelor would be in attendance—thus so would Kaia.

Unfortunately, they were ten minutes into the game, Powell was nowhere in sight, and Kaia could already tell this night was going to drag on forever. To her credit, Harper seemed none too riveted to her boyfriend's pyrotechnic display of athletic prowess. She could barely keep her eyes on the court.

Then both girls yawned at the same instant and, catching sight of each other, burst into grateful laughter. Boredom loves company.

"Want to take a little break?" Harper suggested. "I could really use a cigarette."

At this point, Kaia could really use a lobotomy. But a cigarette would do.

"I'm already out the door," she said, climbing down off her bleacher seat and leading the way through the crowd. Harper had been right: It seemed everyone in town was there. And there, in the front row, looking bored out of his mind, was Powell. Briefly, she considered crossing the room and spicing things up for him— certainly an embarrassing scene in front of this crowd would go a small way toward paying him back for Skiette. But it would also spell the end of them—and Kaia wasn't ready to say good-bye just yet. Even from a distance, he stood out, a splash of wild color against the dullness of the crowd, sex appeal radiating off him in visible waves. Harper caught her staring and sighed appreciatively.

"I know exactly what you're thinking," she said.

If only she did. Snagging a guy as fine as Powell should at the very least have secured Kaia some bragging rights.

"Let's go," Kaia urged her, forcing her gaze away from

Powell's sculpted face and broad chest. She'd deal with him later.

They ducked out a side door and found a dark, empty spot against the side of the gym, lounging in the shadows between two flickering streetlamps.

"Your boyfriend won't miss you in there?" Kaia asked, lighting up and offering Harper a cigarette.

"God, no. This game's been all he could talk about for days. I'm the last thing on his mind."

"You don't look too happy about it," Kaia observed. "That newlywed glow wearing off so soon?"

"Adam and I are *fine*. Perfect, in fact."

Yeah, right. But no way was Kaia letting Harper walk off to pout, leaving her alone without a companion—or a car. What would she do then? Watch the game?

"Whatever," she said agreeably, backing off. "Glad I could help you get what you wanted." It couldn't hurt to remind Harper just whose idea the whole thing had been—without Kaia, Harper and Kane would still be standing with their noses pressed up against the window, watching Adam and Beth's nauseating displays of affection. "And, you know, that it all worked out. Happily ever after and all that. Personally, I'd be a little bored."

"Well, maybe that's because you—" Harper began hotly, then, looking thoughtful, stopped and leaned back against the wall. "Maybe it's this town," she admitted, taking a long drag from the cigarette. "It's enough to drain the life out of anything."

She could say it was the town, but Kaia suspected that the real problem lay a little closer to home, even if Harper didn't realize it. Adam, after all, *was* the town—

Grace's good ol' boy, one of those guys whose life would peak in high school. He'd spend the rest of his life reminiscing about the good old days, not noticing that his beer belly was growing at exactly the same rate that his hair was falling out. Harper didn't look the type to be satisfied with being the good little wifey to a has-been local hero, serving chips 'n' dip to his poker buddies. Why else was she out in the parking lot smoking when she should have been inside, cheering on her man?

But now wasn't the time to bring all that up. Harper wanted to blame her existential angst on the town, and Kaia was only too happy to play along.

"Tell me about it," she complained. "You would think having time off from school would be a good thing, but it just makes it all the more obvious that there's *nothing* to do. I thought I'd be getting out of here for New Year's, but no such luck. Looks like I'll be ringing in the New Year with some hillbillies and flat beer."

Harper laughed. "I'm officially offended by that—but God, what I wouldn't give for a real New Year's, for once. The best we usually get is some illegal firecrackers down at the town dump."

"Pathetic," they said together, rolling their eyes in unison.

"You know what?" Harper asked, spinning to face Kaia, her eyes wide with excitement. "You have a fabulous house. You should have a party."

"Me? I don't know anyone around here."

"But I know everyone—I could help."

"You don't even like me," Kaia pointed out. "And the feeling is mutual."

"True. But you have to admit," Harper said, giving Kaia a sly grin, "we've made a damn good team."

"I'll think about it." The idea of a horde of drunken high schoolers invading Daddy dearest's pristine mansion did have a certain appeal. *Architectural Digest* would likely be somewhat less interested in a feature profile once Kaia had turned the Sellers house into Animal House.

"I'm starving," Harper complained suddenly, breaking into Kaia's reverie of filial delinquency. "How much longer do you think this is going to take?"

"You're the one dating the quarterback."

"Center. I think."

"Whatever—go in there and get him to speed it up a little."

"I don't think that's how it works . . . but I wonder if anyone would notice if we left for a while and found something to eat. . . ."

"Hold that thought," Kaia said, getting the glimmerings of a brilliant idea. "I think I can do you one better."

She whipped out her cell and, taking a few steps away, dialed the number she already knew by heart. "Hello, Guido's? I need to place an order for delivery."

Done. In twenty minutes, their steaming hot pizza would arrive—along with one steaming hot delivery boy.

Now for step two. She dialed again.

"What?" That British accent was so sexy, even when he was sounding annoyed. Especially then.

"I'm outside the gym," Kaia said tersely, knowing he'd be fuming. And knowing he wouldn't hang up. "We need to talk."

Adam cursed under his breath as the ball failed to so much as graze the basket. Airball. He was playing like shit tonight. And he knew exactly why.

"Yo, Kane, good one!" the power forward yelled as Kane stole the ball and landed an easy layup. Another one. There was only one star on the court tonight—and Adam wanted more than anything to bash his cocky, preening face in. It was, to say the least, hurting his concentration.

"Morgan, take a break for a while!" the new coach shouted, sending Lubowski, a lumbering second stringer out in his place. Adam slouched down on the bench with a sigh. If even *Lubowski* was playing better than him, things were worse than he'd thought.

"Dude, looks like you've got some competition this year," the guy next to him on the bench observed. He gestured to the cheerleaders, who were obviously slobbering all over Kane's every move. "Usually they're all about you, man."

"Thanks for the heads up," Adam snapped.

"Hey, take it easy," the guy—Bill, or maybe Will—said cheerfully. "It's not so bad on the bench. I should know, I've been here for years."

So Kane was out there winning the game and Adam was stuck on the bench with some guy who'd never actually touched the ball. He knew it shouldn't matter—he'd always claimed that it didn't matter, the trophies, the news clippings, the girls—but who was he kidding?

He ignored Bill/Will and turned around to scan the crowd, searching for Harper, hoping that the sight of her would remind him of something real, something important, remind him that the game was just that, and nothing more.

But Harper was lost in the crowd somewhere, and the only familiar face he saw was Beth's. He watched her until her wandering eyes met his, then quickly looked away. Back to the court. Back to Kane, who was passing by the bench in a slow jog up the court.

"Nice try tonight," he called in a low voice. "Maybe this weekend I can give you some pointers."

Adam knew he should fight it, should *make* the coach put him back in the game, show Kane he was unfazed. Show Kane that he couldn't have everything, that he didn't always win.

But, instead, he stayed quiet, stayed seated.

The thing was, Kane *did* always win—and Adam was so tired of losing. Maybe it was just better not to fight.

Harper didn't know how they'd had such good fortune, but she was only too happy to enjoy it. When Jack Powell had come storming out of the gym, his face clouded with irritation and a barely contained rage, Harper had been grateful for the quick peek, but assumed he would just walk on by. Instead, inexplicably, he'd stopped to chat with Harper and Kaia—and, just like that, their long and boring night began looking up.

Not that Harper cared about the next lesson in French class or the long-delayed plans to renovate the cafeteria, or whatever it was Kaia was so cheerfully babbling about. Harper was just content to enjoy the scenery. Then again, maybe that was Mr. Powell's motive as well, since he seemed even more disenchanted with the topics of conversation than she was. And he kept sneaking sidelong glances at Harper as if waiting for her to say something. Do something.

Mr. Powell was the first new teacher Haven High had seen in years—and, thanks to his age and obvious sex appeal, rumors had been flying for months. Could they be true? Could the dashing young teacher have his eye on one of his students? Could it be that he was waiting, plotting, hoping to get Harper alone, for a very special student-teacher conference?

Not that she'd ever do anything about it, of course. There was Adam, for one thing—and, for another, hooking up with a teacher was definitely on the wrong side of the sexy/sleazy divide. But that didn't mean she couldn't preen a little under his surreptitious attention, right? Flirt a little, give him the full Harper Grace treatment? You certainly couldn't fault his taste.

"I should be getting back," he finally said, aiming his piercing stare at Kaia. (*Probably wishing she'd go away and leave us alone,* Harper thought smugly.) "Unless there's anything else you ladies need."

"Oh, Mr. Powell, please stay," Kaia simpered, "I really need to talk to you about these new textbook standards you were telling us about. It's so fascinating."

Pathetic, Harper thought. Could she be any more obvious, throwing herself at him like that?

"Well, maybe I didn't mention it before," Mr. Powell began after a pause, "but it's very important that these textbooks follow the *rules.* Otherwise, the school board will just toss them out. After all, one textbook's just as good as another. Don't you think, Harper?"

"What?" Like she was listening. Who could pay attention when he had such adorable dimples? "Uh, sure."

"Oh, I don't know about that," Kaia countered. "I

would think that if a textbook were something really new and different, it might be able to make its own rules. And you know, if one school district didn't want it, another one would be sure to snatch it up."

"And I suppose that in this charming little scenario, the first school board would be sorry?" Mr. Powell asked drily.

"It would feel like quite the fool," Kaia said, imitating his British accent. "It would probably want the textbook back, but, sadly, it would be too late."

Suddenly, Kaia peered into the darkness and waved at an approaching figure who'd just gotten out of his car. "There's our pizza!" she chirped.

"You ordered a pizza?" Harper and Mr. Powell asked together, equally incredulous.

"You *said* you were hungry," Kaia reminded her. "I'll go reel him in," she added, skipping off toward the pizza guy, who was wandering aimlessly in the darkness.

As Kaia's silhouette faded briefly out of sight, Harper turned toward Mr. Powell and realized he was looking intently at her, as if trying to figure something out.

"Well, well, well," she said, her heart pounding in her chest, but her voice steady and light. "Alone at last."

Kaia approached Reed and greeted him with a silent wave. She took the pizza in one hand and, ignoring his confused look, slipped a possessive arm around his waist and led him back toward Harper and Powell.

The pizza had been late, but no matter—she'd been amusing herself by torturing Powell with meaningless small talk, knowing how it made his skin crawl to be seen with her.

"Hi, guys!" she said perkily as she and Reed approached. "Look who brought us the pizza."

Reed—who, despite his greasy GUIDO'S T-shirt and baggy jeans, was looking incredibly tasty—extended a hand toward Harper. Kaia forced herself not to notice the way his unruly long hair brushed the lids of his dark, bottomless eyes. After all, this was business.

"I'm Reed," he said slowly, as if every word had to battle its way through the haze of pot lying between his brain and his mouth. "I think we—"

"They don't care who you are," Kaia interrupted him. She handed the pizza off to Harper, then put her arms around Reed's waist. He was so trim—but so firm. "But *I'm* glad you came," she said, gazing up at Reed—every inch of her attuned to Powell, a few steps away.

"I, uh, didn't know you two knew each other," Harper stuttered.

Kaia touched her hand to Reed's stubbly cheek and glanced over her shoulder.

"Oh, we've gotten to know each other really well these last few days," she said, narrowing her eyes at Powell. "We've gotten very *close.*"

"I should go," Reed said, disengaging himself. He pocketed the money Harper had given him for the pizza and took a step backward.

What's wrong with him? Kaia thought angrily. *Can't he see that I'm throwing myself at him? What is this, performance anxiety? He's only into me when we're in some freakish, secluded spot all by ourselves?*

She shivered at the memory. She'd promised herself she wouldn't think of those nights again.

Focus, she reminded herself. *And don't let him go.*

"Reed," she called sweetly, and he turned around again to face her. "You forgot your tip."

She stepped toward him and gave him a soft, chaste kiss on the lips.

Behind her, she heard a gasp. And knew without looking that it wasn't Harper. Perfect.

Then Reed put his arms around her and pulled her closer, and their chaste kiss turned into something else. Long, deep, his fingers crawling down her back, their bodies fusing—and then it was over.

Reed walked away, into the shadows, and Kaia watched him go. Watched long after his figure had disappeared.

Eventually, behind her, Jack Powell cleared his throat.

Kaia had almost forgotten he was there.

chapter

9

"Come on, Kane, where are we going?" Beth peered out the window at the desert landscape speeding by as if the bumpy, arid land on either side would offer some kind of clue. But there was nothing out there but scraggly Joshua trees, distant hills, and the occasional billboard for an XXX strip club a mere fifty miles away.

"How many times have you asked me that?" Kane asked, glancing over at her with bemusement and then turning back to the road.

Counting this morning, when he'd begged her to ditch her applications for the day and take a road trip? Counting the hour in the grocery store buying water and picnic preparations, and then the hour and a half on the road?

"About thirty," she guessed, blushing.

"Add another zero and you'll be closer," Kane said, shaking his head. "And what have I told you each and every time?"

"'It's a surprise,'" she quoted dutifully.

"So? Can't you come up with a new question?"

"Okay." Beth smiled mischievously. "Are we there yet?"

As the sound of laughter filled the car, Beth leaned her head back against the leather seat and closed her eyes. Maybe Kane was right and she should just relax, see where the day took them. She'd never been very good with surprises—but, thanks to Kane, she was learning.

"Patience," Kane counseled. "All good things come to those who wait. At least . . ." he put his hand on her leg and began rubbing her inner thigh. "You did."

Powell's apartment was worth about what he was paying for it. Which meant it was slightly cozier than a soggy cardboard box, with better insulation. The rusted aluminum siding covering the face of the house was slathered with peeling grayish-yellow paint—and the inside wasn't much more appealing. Powell's tiny monthly rent check paid for a bedroom about twice the size of his bed, a bathroom (leaky shower, no tub), and a living room-dining room-entry hall-kitchenette area that offered slightly more elbow room than the front seat of a car.

In only a few short weeks, Kaia had memorized the shape and position of every water stain on the avocado green wallpaper, and every crack in the vomit-colored ceiling. The only thing she wasn't sick of yet was the view, and that was only because she'd never seen it—Powell made her stay away from the windows.

Or, at least, he had in the past. Lying back on his bed and watching him pace angrily back and forth across the small room, Kaia could almost feel the balance of power shifting in her direction.

"A pizza boy, Kaia?"

He couldn't get over it. Not just the idea of her in someone else's arms, but the idea that he'd been sharing her with a delivery boy, of all people. Powell was a snob at heart. It was something they had in common.

"A ski bunny, *Jack*?"

"So this is revenge, then? A little juvenile, don't you think?"

Kaia just shrugged. "Not everything I do is about you," she pointed out. "Sometimes I like to have a little fun."

"I told you, no high school boys," Powell snapped. "We agreed on that at the outset."

Kaia sat up and leaned forward, and in spite of himself, Powell's eyes followed her cleavage.

"You want me to go?" she asked, pretending to gather her belongings. "Fine with me."

"I suppose"—Powell sat down beside her—"I could be persuaded to give you a second chance." He began kneading his hands against her bare shoulders, exploring the contours of her neck, her back. "Provided you give up your pizza boy."

"And you?" Kaia asked, walking her fingers lightly up his bare arm. "Will you be giving up Snow White?"

"That wasn't part of our deal," Powell said.

Kaia slowly unbuttoned her shirt, revealing a lacy red bra. "New deal. You play, I play."

"I don't like to share," Powell said in a low, dangerous voice. He wrapped his arms around her from behind and squeezed tight. Almost too tight.

"What a coincidence," Kaia whispered, leaning her head back against him so that her lips were nearly pressed against his face. "Neither do I."

Harper didn't believe in failure. So when her parents took off for a day of antiquing (read: spending too much for other people's discarded clutter at roadside flea markets), she was ready. Without a job to stand in her way, she had all the time in the world to set things up—and when Adam finally showed up, she knew he'd be blown away.

"Uh, Harper?" he asked, hesitating in her doorway. "What's going on?"

"Do you like it?" she asked eagerly, stepping aside so he could get the full view. "I did it for you. Well . . . for us."

"It's, uh . . . wow."

With only a few hours of hard work (Harper's least favorite kind), the living room had been transformed into a winter wonderland. The electric fireplace roared and crackled as if it held a real pile of logs, the walls were dotted with crudely cut paper snowflakes, and Bing Crosby's "White Christmas" blared from the stereo. (Good thing her parents were addicted to cheesy holiday music—they had a whole shelf of this crap.)

"But . . . why?" Adam asked as Harper guided him to a couch piled high with blankets. She'd turned the air conditioner on full blast, and offered him a steaming cup of hot chocolate.

"I thought we were just hanging out, Harper—you know, low-key. After last night at the game—"

"Oh, don't think about that," Harper said quickly, ruffling his hair. The last thing he needed now was to dwell on his inadequacy.

"I thought we could both use a little treat," Harper

explained. "After all, the ski trip"—how to put it delicately?—"didn't really go as planned. So I thought we could have a 'do-over.'"

"A 'do-over'?"

"You remember, when we used to play four-square in the driveway, and you'd try to cheat—"

"I never cheated," he protested indignantly.

"Whatever you say," she said, leaning against him. "Anyway, if something, or *someone,* interrupted normal play, we'd just forget it ever happened and start that turn all over again. A do-over."

"Have I ever told you you're adorable?" Adam asked, and she knew she had him.

"Not nearly enough."

It was the romantic getaway from hell. Or rather, *to* hell, if hell was anything like the dark, cluttered space with half-empty pizza boxes dotting the floor, also known as Kane's brother's apartment. Aaron Geary and a few of his friends sat around the room on makeshift chairs—mostly milk crates and rusty lawn furniture—while Kane and Beth shared a sagging beanbag that was leaking tiny white plastic beads all over the floor.

What more could a girl ask for?

"No thanks," she said firmly as a giant bong—the first she'd ever seen in person—was again passed around the circle. Beth had been trying all afternoon to breathe shallowly so as to ingest as little of the pot fumes as possible. Still, the smoke was giving her a raging headache. And her patience was wearing thin.

"Can I talk to you for a second?" she hissed at Kane,

who was bopping his head along to the Jimmy Buffett sound track—on an endless loop—totally oblivious to her discomfort.

She pulled him up off the beanbag chair and led him down a dark hallway into Aaron's bedroom.

"Have fun, lovebirds!" Aaron shouted. "I just changed the sheets!"

What luck.

Beth grimaced and tried not to touch anything in the room—a thick layer of dust covered everything, from the rickety futon to the dilapidated dresser. A few empty vodka bottles served as the only decoration.

"Having a good time, babe?" Kane asked, leaning in to her. Unsteady on his feet from an afternoon overflowing with beer and pot, he almost toppled over.

Beth recoiled from his touch and turned her head away from his foul pot breath. "No, I'm not having fun," she informed him testily. "Why did you bring me here?"

"What do you mean?" Kane sat down on the futon and tried, unsuccessfully, to pull her down onto his lap. "It's a road trip—it was supposed to be fun."

"Kane, you dragged me out here into the middle of nowhere to waste the day in your brother's pit of an apartment with his burnout friends. How, exactly, was that supposed to be fun?"

"Lighten up, Manning—do you always have to be so uptight?"

From the look in his bloodshot eyes, she could tell that it had just slipped out—but she could also tell that he'd meant it.

Kane stood and tried to put his arms around her, but she pushed him away.

"I'm leaving," Beth said, with as much dignity as she could muster. "It's obvious you'll have more *fun* without me." She meant it to sound cruel, angry—but maybe it was true. Maybe she *was* uptight. Hadn't Adam always implied as much, even if he'd never come right out and said it? Why couldn't she just hang out and enjoy herself for a few hours, turn her brain off, relax?

"Beth, wait," he begged, grabbing her arms and pulling her toward him. "Don't—I shouldn't have said that. I didn't mean it."

"Yes, you did," she said quietly, not meeting his eyes.

"I *didn't*. I love spending time with you. Of course you're fun."

"Yeah, right." Kane was a champion sweet-talker, but it was going to take more than charisma to fix this.

"Look, to be honest, I knew this wasn't your thing," he finally admitted, sitting down again. "You can go, if you want. I wouldn't blame you. I never should have brought you out here."

It wasn't the words so much as the uncharacteristic note of sincerity—and, more than that, vulnerability—that gave her pause. Made her stay. She sat down beside him. "So why did you bring me here?"

He looked down at his hands, which were playing aimlessly with the fraying edge of his brother's comforter. "It's stupid."

"Too bad," she said, relishing the rare sensation of having control over the conversation. "What's going on?"

"I just . . . wanted you to meet my brother," Kane

mumbled. "I wanted to show you off to him," he added, putting an arm around her. Beth didn't resist. "To show him . . ." His voice drifted off.

"What?" Beth asked gently. She took his hand.

"You're the first girl I've ever introduced to my family. I'm . . . proud of myself, I guess you could say, for dating such an amazing girl. That someone like you would be with me."

"Kane . . ."

"I sound like a total loser."

"No!" she protested. It was possibly the sweetest thing anyone had ever said to her—and to think she'd almost walked out before giving him a chance. It was just like her, Beth berated herself—always judging, always planning, never willing to take things at face value, to just relax into the moment. The only good news was that it was never too late to change.

"We should get back out there," Kane suggested, obviously embarrassed.

"What's your hurry?" Beth asked, pulling him toward her into a kiss. Suddenly she didn't care about the dirty comforter or the sagging futon, the spiderwebs in the corner of the room or the deadbeats eavesdropping on the other side of the door. She only cared about Kane—and she was ready to show him just how much.

Adam tried to remember what the Web site had cautioned him about calming down, releasing his stress.

Relax, he told himself. *Enjoy the moment. Enjoy Harper.*

So he tried. He kissed her, rubbed her back, closed his eyes, and pulled off her shirt. She was beautiful, she had an amazing body—but it just wasn't . . . it just wasn't happening. The whole thing felt so fake and scripted: put this hand here, that hand there, think sexy thoughts. And the damn Christmas music in the background wasn't helping.

"Mmm, Adam, I love the smell of your hair," Harper mumbled, her face buried in his neck.

It was the same thing Beth always used to say.

And that was all it took—her face, unbidden, swam up in his mind's eye, smiling mockingly at him. And there was Kane, suddenly next to her, kissing her, both of them laughing at Adam, at his stupidity, his weakness. His inadequacy.

Get out of my head, he wanted to scream, feeling like the walls were closing in. He hadn't slept the night before, going over and over the game in his head, seeing Kane's face as he scored the winning shot while Adam rode the bench. All he'd wanted to do today was get away, forget all his problems. But here was Harper, pushing him, reminding him of everything he couldn't do, couldn't be . . . it was all too much—

"Stop!" he finally said harshly, pushing her away, feeling like his head was going to explode.

"What is it?" she asked, lightly touching his cheek. "What's wrong?"

"It's all this, this shit," Adam said, throwing wide his arms to encompass the decorations, the music, all of it. "This is the last thing I want to think about, Harper—I thought we agreed to just forget that night ever happened. And then you go and throw it in my face?"

"I just thought, if we tried again. . . ."

He wasn't angry at her, he knew that. But he was too

ashamed to admit it—too ashamed to admit that he'd failed her once again. What kind of teenage guy was he? Where were all those raging hormones when you needed them? Instead, here he was, stuck with a horny girlfriend, lukewarm hot chocolate, and a limp dick.

"I have to go," he said quickly—and it was, suddenly, a physical need not to be there anymore, not to have her look at him with those pitying eyes. He was too proud to accept her pity—and too terrified of what would happen when her pity turned to scorn. What if, after a few days of this, a week, she got sick of it? Of him? What if she told her friends?

This is Harper, he reminded himself. *You can trust her.*

"I'm sorry," he said sincerely. But he couldn't touch her. "I really am. I'm not mad. I'm just—" He stood up and backed away. "I just need to go. I'll call you."

He was out the door before she could say anything.

True, it was Harper, and he could trust her more than anyone—but how much was that?

After Beth, after Kane, he wasn't sure he believed in trust anymore. And if betrayal was inevitable, maybe it was just better to be alone.

She'd bought it. He'd known the family card was just the right one to play—and once again, his instincts had proven infallible. Poor Kane, so reluctant to open up, so eager to show off his beloved girl to his beloved brother. All they'd done in Aaron's room was kiss, but Kane wondered. If only he'd thought of the teary-eyed routine back on the ski trip, when they'd had a room to themselves and all the time in the world.

And yet—it hadn't been a total lie, had it? Why else had he brought Beth along on this little excursion, knowing ahead of time it would likely be more trouble than it was worth. Wasn't he trying to show her off to his brother, prove that Kane had managed to get something Aaron never had?

Kane shrugged it off—he didn't care to plumb the depths of his subconscious. Leave that to the ladies.

"We can take off in a minute," he whispered to her. She was pretending to be deeply engrossed in his brother's explanation of the differing merits of Grand Theft Auto and Gran Turismo 4. What a girl.

She nodded slightly, and Kane patted her on the shoulder before standing up and catching the eye of one of the guys across the room—a lanky, scraggly haired college dropout who went only by the name of "C." He jerked his head slightly toward the door and headed outside, knowing C would follow. Time to accomplish what he'd come for.

"Yo, Kane, good to see you," C said in a raspy voice, once they were alone. He bumped fists with Kane, then frowned. "I'm just sorry you came all this way for nothing."

"What are you talking about?" Kane had, after much thought, come up with the perfect present for Beth— something to make their New Year's Eve a night neither would soon forget. And C had promised that, as always, he'd be able to hook Kane up.

"Man, sorry, I thought I had enough, but you know how it is."

"No, I don't know how it is. You couldn't tell me this before I drove all the way up here?"

"Forgot." C shrugged. "What can you do?"

"You've got *nothing*?" Kane asked in frustration. "Absolutely nothing?"

"Well"—C's mouth widened into a rat-like grin—"you gotta keep a little something, just in case."

"I'll take it."

"No way, man, that's my emergency supply."

"Double the usual price," Kane suggested. This was an emergency.

"No deal. It's not about the money, bro. It's not for sale."

"Everything's for sale," Kane countered, a philosophy that had yet to fail him. "There must be something you want, something only I can get for you."

"Actually . . ." C chewed the corner of his lip. "There may be something—but you're not going to like it."

C spit it out—and under other circumstances, Kane might have laughed in his face and walked away. But today was C's lucky day.

"It just so happens that you've named the one thing I'm able to deliver," Kane said triumphantly. He could already see all the details falling into place. It was amoral, it was underhanded, and it was going to make someone *very* unhappy, but it would get Kane what he needed.

And in the end, what else mattered?

chapter

10

"Do you know what time it is?" Harper asked groggily, slumping back against her pillow.

"Did I wake you, princess?" Even through the phone, Harper could hear the false note in Kane's syrupy sympathetic voice. And after the week she'd been having, she wasn't in the mood.

"Yes."

"Good—because you've got to get going or you'll be late."

"Late for what?" Harper was on the verge of hanging up. It was way too early in the morning for one of Kane's mind games.

"You've got a date."

"Trust me, I don't." Not that she wanted to think about that. She hadn't heard from Adam since he'd run off from her ill-conceived winter extravaganza.

"You do now. His name is C. And you're going to love him." Kane laughed. "Actually, you're going to hate him—but you're going, anyway."

"I'm hanging up now," Harper warned him impatiently.

"Look, he graduated a couple years ago from Haven and apparently he had a huge crush on you. God knows why."

"I'll ignore that," Harper snapped.

"You blew him off."

"Imagine that."

"But for some reason, he's been longing for you ever since . . . kind of sweet, when you think about it. You know, in a crazed-stalker kind of way."

"Charming," Harper drawled—a bit intrigued, in spite of herself.

"Since the poor guy's been pining away for you so pitifully, I told him you'd drive up there and have lunch with him today."

Harper almost dropped the phone. "You did *what*? Why would I possibly do that?"

"Out of the goodness of your heart?" Kane suggested.

"Funny, I seem to have misplaced that."

"Then need I remind you of the favor you owe me?" Harper gripped the phone tightly—she should have known that nothing from Kane came without strings attached. "I'm calling it in."

"Kane, lending me money doesn't give you the right to pimp me out to your deadbeat friends," she pointed out.

"Oh, get off it, Grace, it's lunch, not an afternoon rendezvous at the Whore Hotel. All you need to do is drive up there, let the guy buy you lunch and pay you a few compliments, then drive home again. And, oh yeah," he added, affecting a casual tone, "he has something for me, a package, so if you can bring it back with you, that'd be great."

"And if I say no?" Harper asked.

"Have you cashed the check yet?"

Damn.

No.

"I can always stop payment."

Harper wanted to throw the phone across the room. He could be such an asshole sometimes. All the time.

"But hey, I wouldn't do that to a friend," he smarmed. "I'm more than happy to do you a favor, because that's what friends do for each other. *Right?*"

"His name is 'C'?" Harper asked. "What's it stand for?"

"Nothing—just C."

Of course.

"And he's in college with your brother?"

"He *was* . . . ," Kane clarified.

"He graduated already?" she asked—a prodigy wouldn't be too bad.

"He . . . moved on."

No name and no future—this just kept getting better and better. Still . . . he was an older guy, and he found her desirable, which was more than she could say for the other man in her life. And it's not like it would be a *real* date or anything, so Adam would have nothing to complain about. (Not that he would ever find out.)

"And you won't have to pay interest on the loan," Kane added hopefully.

Free lunch and an interest-free loan, all for spending a few hours letting some guy tell her how beautiful she was?

"Gotta go, Kane—looks like I've got myself a date."

"I have a proposition for you, *mon chérie,*" Powell said, dipping his Oreo in a glass of milk and taking a bite. Their first night together, they had dined on fine wine and imported cheeses, Kaia remembered with a sweet pang of nostalgia. Now they'd been reduced to early morning milk and cookies. When did things go from scandalous to seedy to suburban?

"I'm listening."

"What are you up to on New Year's Eve?" he asked.

Kaia maintained a neutral expression, but inside, she was beaming. He wanted to spend New Year's with her? It looked like her little power play was already taking off.

"I've got this party to go to," he began, and she looked at him in surprise. A couple weeks ago he'd chastised her for smiling at him in the high school hallway. Now he wanted to take her out in public?

"I can't get out of it," he complained, "but I should be home by one or two, and I thought—"

"What?" she snapped, comprehension dawning. "That I'd have nothing better to do on New Year's Eve than sit around and wait for your booty call? Just how pathetic do you think I am?"

"You didn't seem to have a problem with it tonight," he pointed out, "or any other night, that I can recall."

"Well, it just so happens that on *that* night, I've got something else to do."

Powell sat up in bed and looked at her suspiciously. "Something else—or *someone* else?"

His jealous tone was confirmation enough that her little show with Reed had done the trick. But it looked like he hadn't quite learned his lesson—not if he still expected her to be sitting by the phone at all hours, waiting for his call. She'd stay faithful to their pact—but that didn't mean he owned her.

"I'm having a party of my own," she explained, deciding in that instant to make it true. "But if I get bored, later, maybe *I'll* call *you*. But don't count on it—my parties aren't often boring."

"Well then, all the more reason to get my fill of you while I can," he said, tugging her close.

"I'm leaving now," she informed him. Time to make him beg.

"Now, now, don't go away mad. *J'ai besoin de toi, mon amoureuse. Reste avec moi—je t'implore.*"

I need you, lover. Stay with me—I beg of you.

He knew she couldn't resist him when he spoke to her in French, his British accent submerged in the soft syllables of longing.

The language of love, they called it. But there was nothing pure and nothing loving in his tone—only naked desire. Need.

And nothing appealed to Kaia more than that.

"Je suis ici," she whispered, falling into his arms. *"Et je suis tout tiens."*

I'm here.

And I'm all yours.

Forty miles was a long way to drive for lunch. She made a mental note to have Kane repay her for the gas.

Harper had a lot of time to make mental to do lists, since it's not like she was listening to "C" prattle on about his collection of Jay-Z MP3s or the garage band he and his friends were planning to start . . . any day now. (C had a lot of plans, apparently—and not a whole lot to show for them except a few tattoos and a thriving business in supplying illegal substances to desperate high school kids.)

She remembered him now. Back in Grace, C had been Charles Dallas, aka "Chuckie D," who'd bounced around from group to group looking for his niche. He'd dropped his junior high Dungeons and Dragons clan, washed out of the rapper wannabes, and finally settled in with a bunch of deadbeat dealers who spent most of high school in the parking lot, swapping stories about what they'd do when they escaped from Grace. Most of them never had.

"You want dessert?" C asked, appearing not to notice the fact that Harper's plate—piled high with a rancid "buffalo" burger and stale chips—was untouched. She wasn't about to eat anything in this dive, a dingy roadside diner decorated with old license plates and populated by a few locals who were drinking their lunch before heading home to watch the game and work on their trucks. They'd agreed to meet here, halfway between their two towns, but Harper realized now that she should have sucked it up and driven the full eighty miles—at least C lived in a college town, with other people, other buildings, anything other than the dusty gray emptiness that surrounded them on all sides.

"Thanks, anyway," she said, in the same monotonous tone she'd been using the whole meal. "I'm full."

"I had in mind a little something *off* the menu," C said, tapping his jacket pocket and giving her a toothy grin. Harper so did not want to know what was in there.

"Raincheck?" she requested wearily. "I'm good. Really."

"You sure are," he agreed, looking her up and down with appreciation. "I still can't believe I'm here with you. I mean, it's fucking Harper Grace! In a dump like this, with a loser like me. I must be dreaming."

Harper allowed herself a small smile. A compliment was a compliment, no matter who delivered it.

"The guys are never going to believe this," he crowed, tossing a wad of cash down on the table.

"The guys?" Harper asked as C pulled out her chair and helped her up—so chivalrous for a deadbeat.

"Oh, yeah. There's a bunch of us up there from Haven, and we all remember you. I mean, dude, you're *Harper Grace.*"

Harper pushed a stray hair out of her eyes, preening under his longing gaze. So she had a little fan club up there, did she? Feeling a sudden burst of goodwill for C, she laced her arm through his as they strolled the gravelly path toward the parking lot. "So, C," she said sweetly, "what is it, exactly, that makes me so memorable?"

As C began rhapsodizing—in his admittedly limited vocabulary—about her many divine attributes, Harper's mood lifted. So this is what it felt like to be worshipped. She'd almost forgotten.

". . . and, you know, you're just totally sexy. I mean, *hot.*"

"My boyfriend doesn't seem to think so," Harper muttered—then stopped walking, appalled she had said it aloud.

"Any guy who doesn't think you're the hottest thing he's ever seen is fucking crazy," C exclaimed.

Harper turned to look at C, really look at him. He wasn't *so* bad looking, if you ignored the crooked smile and the way one eye seemed to wander off when he tried to meet your gaze. And the bad skin. And the greasy hair.

Okay, he was a dog. But he was looking at her like a hungry puppy who'd just spotted a Salisbury steak. And Harper decided to put him out of his misery.

"You think 'the guys' won't believe we had lunch together?" Harper asked, putting a hand on each of his shoulders and pulling him toward her. "Wait until they hear about this."

It was a wet, sloppy kiss, short on romance, overly long on bad breath and C's thrusting tongue. But as he pressed himself against her and Hoovered his way across her face, sucking and slobbering like an animal, Harper could feel just how much he wanted her. At least someone did.

Adam skimmed through the online photo gallery without paying much attention. He'd almost deleted the e-mail without opening it. Some guy on the team was dating a girl who was obsessed with photographically documenting every moment of their senior year, which meant periodic mass e-mails filled with memories Adam would just as soon forget. And the ski trip was at the top of the list.

But something had made him save the e-mail. And this afternoon, something had made him open it. Most were pictures of people he barely knew, didn't care about—he and Harper had done their best to stay away from the crowd, and that meant away from the camera. But there were a few shots that made him pause. Harper, bundled in her thick green coat, leaning against Adam's shoulder. Adam, tossing a snowball at Harper, grabbing her hand as she tried to escape.

There'd been some good moments, he reminded himself.

And so he was smiling when he clicked open the next photo. When the picture of Beth and Kane, tangled in each other's arms, exploded across the screen.

Adam slammed his fist down on the keyboard and shut off the monitor. But the image stayed with him, burned into his brain, like those other images, two months earlier. Every time he saw them together, it was as if it were the first time, and he was hit with the same blast of shock, disgust, and fury. And every time, there was only one thought that calmed him down, one person who could remind him that not everything in his life was ugly and twisted. No matter how awkward things were between them, she was still the only one he could talk to. The only one he wanted to talk to.

He dialed her number, and waited.

The phone rang and rang.

He didn't leave a message.

It was a long drive home, and Harper had plenty of time to think. Too much.

She'd kissed another guy, she realized, the gritty, sour taste of C still in her mouth. No wonder Adam didn't want her—deep inside, he could tell what kind of person she was. A quitter. A cheater. Adam had no idea what she was really like—but some part of him must sense it, Harper realized, must know that she wasn't good enough for him.

She'd never felt so low—and then she got home. And things got worse.

"I'm skipping dinner," Harper mumbled to her mother, blowing by her on the way upstairs to her room.

"Hon, wait a second. Your father and I have something we want to say to you."

Uh-oh.

In the history of Grace family relations, that had never been good.

Already halfway up the stairs, Harper slunk back down and followed her mother into the parlor. Her father was already there, perched stiffly on an overstuffed blue chair he only used to entertain guests. The whole room was, in fact, used only under special circumstances—the Graces' large house, left over from boom times, had far more space than their small family could use. Often, Harper felt like the house was mocking her, reminding her of the life she was supposed to have.

"Sit down, Harper," her father requested sternly.

She did as he said, stomach sinking, mind racing to figure out what it was she might have done.

"Harper, as you know, the family's been going through some tough times lately," her father began.

As if she needed a reminder. "And, as you know, we decided that this ski trip stretched our budget too much, and that if you really wanted to go—"

"I'd have to pay for it myself," Harper finished with him. Old news. Unless—what if they had somehow found out that she'd quit her job?

"We've been watching you very carefully these last few weeks, and we want to tell you—"

Here it came.

"We're so very proud of you, Harper."

"What?"

"We know how much you hated the idea of having a job, honey," her mother explained. "And to see you going off to work every day—"

"On your winter vacation, no less!" her father chimed in.

"We just want you to know, sweetie, that we really respect what you've shown you can do."

"Your mother and I have talked it over and we've decided that, as a reward, if you make enough to pay us back for half the ski trip, we'll cover the other half."

"I-I don't know what to say," Harper stuttered, feeling her lies bubbling up inside of her, along with her lunch. "Thank you?"

"You don't have to thank us, honey." Her mother came over to offer her a warm hug. "We're just so happy to have a daughter who's not afraid of a little hard work. I always knew that if you really put your mind to something, you'd be able to accomplish anything."

Harper felt like shit. Lower than shit. Her parents were treating her like a superhero—some hero. What were her special powers: the ability to destroy relationships in a single bound? The power to make her real, lying, cheating self disappear?

Her parents had certainly bought in to her secret identity—and, for the moment, so had Adam. But it was a small town, and she wasn't invincible. How long would it be, Harper wondered, before the truth came out?

"I can't wait to see who you really are."

Miranda couldn't forget his words, couldn't stop repeating them to herself. They were so exciting—and terrifying. What if he took one look and ran away in the other direction? What if he was expecting someone totally different: someone tall, skinny, confident? And instead he ended up with Miranda. Who wouldn't be disappointed? Who wouldn't feel cheated?

Beneath all the self-deprecation, Miranda still found time to wonder—what was *he* really like? What kind of guy needed to pick up girls on the Internet? Was there such a thing as a cool, artsy, intelligent, single guy? Or was ReadItAndWeep just a troll—a pale, gawky, weirdo just looking to get laid?

What were the odds that he would be good enough for her—and if he was, that she would be good enough for him?

A million to one seemed a cautious guess.

And yet—sometimes, Miranda reminded herself, you've got to take a chance. So she'd made the date. She'd gotten dressed in her best casual—but hopefully hot—outfit: slimming dark jeans, with a lacy, see-through black top; brushed her long, lank hair into something approximating silky sheen; dug out her tallest pair of high heels; and taken one last look in the mirror. Two days on the slopes had failed to tan her pale skin, but in certain lights, she had an arguably healthy glow. Good enough.

She took a deep breath and set off for Bourquin's Coffee Shop to meet the man of her dreams. Or, at least, of her e-mails.

She'd just left her house when the phone rang. Miranda almost didn't answer. If it was him, backing out at the last minute, did she really want to know? And then she remembered: They hadn't exchanged phone numbers. She was safe. Or so she thought.

"Hello?"

"Rand . . . Rand, I need you."

"Harper? Are you—what's going on?"

Harper's voice sounded strange, muffled, her words broken by hiccuping pauses.

"I don't know what's wrong with me, Rand, I just— I'm a terrible person, my life is shit, I'm—"

"Slow down, Harper, please, just—calm down." Was she crying? Impossible. "What's wrong?"

"I can't tell you. . . . It doesn't matter. I just—I can't be alone right now. Rand—can I come over?"

"Uh . . . I'm kind of . . . out, right now, Harper."

"Oh." She said it in such a small, pitiful voice, Miranda cringed. "Okay, I guess I'll just talk to you"—she sniffed and, Miranda thought, might even have whimpered— "later. Bye."

"Harper, wait!" Miranda sighed, weighing her options. She could hang up. This was probably just another Harper Grace melodrama—it would blow over in a few hours. And, given the number of times Harper had ditched her in her time of need, there would be a certain poetic justice in leaving her hanging. Maybe it was time to put her own life first, for once.

On the other hand . . . this was Harper, her best friend. And that had to mean something, right? She'd never heard Harper like this before, vulnerable, needy. And, Miranda had to admit, it felt pretty good. Like Harper had finally figured out how desperately she needed the kind of friendship that only Miranda could provide.

"I'm about five minutes from home, Harper," she said, hoping she wouldn't regret this. "You can come over whenever you need to."

"Thanks, Rand, you're the best. Really. I don't know what I'd do without you."

It felt so good to hear those words—almost good enough to make Miranda forget about the mystery man who was sitting in the back of the coffee shop waiting for the girl with red hair and a spunky sense of humor. The girl who would never show up, who didn't have a number to call. She'd e-mail him to explain, she promised herself. And he'd understand. He would have to.

Four hours later, holding Harper's hair as she leaned over the toilet, puking up a night's worth of Screwdrivers, Miranda was no longer so sure she wanted this best friend gig after all.

Harper had shown up half drunk and, after an hour or so at Miranda's, had gone the rest of the way. Her parents were, thankfully, out for the night and her sister was sleeping over a friend's house—so there was no one but Miranda to witness Harper's meltdown, and no one but Miranda to clean up the mess.

The most frustrating thing was that Harper wouldn't tell her anything about what was wrong. Their conversations wandered around in lazy circles, as unable to walk a straight line as Harper was.

"He doesn't love me," Harper would sob.

"Who?"

"Adam. He thinks I'm a slut. I *am* a slut. He hates me."

"What are you talking about? Of course he doesn't—"

"Everyone hates me. I'm going to be all alone. When they find out what I did."

"Who?"

"My parents. Adam. Beth. You. Everyone. You'll all hate me. You should hate me. I'm horrible."

"But what did you do?" Miranda asked, again and again, mystified.

"Nothing. Everything. I don't know—it doesn't matter. Nothing matters, because he doesn't want me. He doesn't love me."

And then the whole thing started all over again.

Until the puking began. All that vodka on an empty stomach—Harper should have known better. Or Miranda should have known better for her.

Finally, Harper stood up. Slow, unsteady on her feet, and stumbling back to Miranda's room, flopping down, facefirst, on the bed. Miranda forced her to turn over on her side, forced her to drink a little water.

"What will I do without you, Rand?" Harper asked, moaning with the effort of having to move.

"You'll never have to find out," Miranda said soothingly, taking off Harper's shoes and covering her with a light blanket. She settled into a chair by the bed, planning to stay up and watch Harper breathe. Just to make sure everything was all right.

"No, you'll leave me, when you find out," Harper whimpered. "You all will."

"Never," Miranda swore.

"No." Harper sighed, and closed her eyes. "Soon."

chapter

11

In 500 words or less, describe something about yourself that makes you proud.

I never knew I was afraid of heights until I was standing at the top of the mountain, looking down. The hill looked like a ninety-degree angle—and it looked bottomless. I didn't want to admit it at the time, but I was scared. I was terrified. I didn't know what I was getting myself into. I just knew I had to do it. No matter what, I had to try. So I pushed myself to the very edge, I counted to three, and then I tipped my skis forward—and I was flying!

I'm proud of myself for making it down the hill in one piece, but that's not what this essay's about. I'm proud of myself for going back up to the top and trying all over again, even though I was just as terrified the second time around, and the third.

But that's not what this essay is about either.

Because what I'm most proud of is the fact that I went down at all, that first time. I looked over the edge, and I was scared out of my mind. But I did it, anyway.

I'm a quiet girl, and I live a quiet life. Not boring, not dull—just quiet. "She's a nice girl"—people say that a lot. Also: "She always does the right thing." "Always does what she's supposed to do." And I'm proud of that, too.

But that's not me, or at least, not all of me. Because somewhere in me, there's someone else, someone loud and exciting. Someone looking for mountains to ski down, for all kinds of new experiences, no matter how scary they may seem at first. Every once in a while, something inside of me wants to take a chance, and do something that no one would ever expect. Trying new things, facing your fears, taking a risk—it's not always easy. I'm still finding my way. But I know that college will be the perfect place to learn. The way I see it, going to college is like the ultimate ski slope. It's terrifying, the great unknown—but you know that if you can just make that first jump off the edge, you'll have an amazing ride.

I'm ready to jump.

Kane looked up from the page, and Beth watched him expectantly, her heart in her throat.

"So? What do you think?" she asked, not sure she wanted to hear the answer. After days of being totally blocked, she'd been suddenly inspired and had stayed up all night writing. Kane was the first person to read it. And if he thought it was stupid—and, reading it over for the hundredth time, it sounded stupider and stupider to her—she didn't know what she would do.

"You're a genius!" he exclaimed, taking her in his arms. "It's brilliant."

"Really? You're not just saying that? If it's terrible, I'd rather know now and—"

"It's amazing," he insisted, cutting her off with a kiss. "You're amazing. This is exactly the kind of corny bullshit colleges love to hear. You're going to have them eating out of your hand."

"It's not—" Beth stopped, unsure how to explain that she'd meant every word, cheesy as it may seem. But she didn't want Kane to think less of her, and wipe that admiring look off his face. And it didn't really matter if he'd totally misunderstood her intentions, if he believed the essay or not. He *liked* it—that was the important thing.

Right?

Kaia read over the invitation a few times and then clicked send, fully satisfied. Harper had supplied her with a list of e-mail addresses and assured her she'd put the word out that all the right people should show up—and all the wrong ones should stay home.

It had been easier than she'd expected to snag her father's permission for the party (sneaking out of the house was one thing—sneaking one hundred people *in* might have proven somewhat more difficult, so she'd gone the more official route). Of course, she'd billed it as an elegant cocktail hour, something to keep her and her "friends" out of trouble on the big night. But after threatening him with her other suggestion—spending some quality time together, just the two of them—she suspected he would have agreed to anything. Keith Sellers cancel his annual New Year's trip to Cabo to spend the night doing the "Father Knows Best" thing with his delinquent daughter? It was about as likely as her mother popping in for a surprise visit.

No, Kaia was on her own—as usual—and, courtesy of Daddy, had a nice chunk of change with which to make this party worthy of Harper's hype. The servants were holding on to the cash, of course. Kaia's father had figured that with his credit card in hand, she'd be on the next plane back to New York. (And he was right.) Besides, better that the help hold on to the purchasing power, since they'd be the ones doing all the purchasing.

She'd hit only one snag so far in the planning process: the list of invitees. True, Harper had supplied most of the names, but there was a wild card: Reed Sawyer. Kaia had toyed with the idea of inviting him—after all, it would be nice to have someone to kiss at midnight. Someone dark, mysterious, and handsome, whose lips lit her on fire. . . .

And that's where she'd cut herself off. Reed was a toy, a plaything, something to use and discard once she'd gotten what she needed out of him. Seeing him again, thinking about him any longer, would just tempt her to forget all that—and if she wanted to keep Powell around, she couldn't afford to forget.

Reed didn't know it yet, but his new year was going to be Kaia-free.

Lucky thing, Kane supposed, that Adam's mother had answered the phone. Adam probably would have hung up before Kane could get a word out. Mrs. Morgan—like most women—was far more accommodating.

Maybe he'd been inspired by Beth's corny essay. Or maybe, much as he hated to admit it, by Beth herself, those clear, shining eyes, trusting, open, always ready for a challenge. If she was willing to try something new, to take a chance—and Kane was hoping that he'd correctly interpreted her words to mean she was finally willing to take a real chance on him—so could he.

So after leaving her house, he'd called Adam—and since Adam's mother had pulled a Benedict Arnold, Kane now knew exactly where to find him.

It was the first place he would have looked.

It was a cool day, but Adam was playing shirtless, sweaty enough that Kane knew he'd been on the court all day.

"Practice makes perfect, eh?" he called out as he approached, wincing at the sarcastic note in his voice. He could never stop himself from goading Adam on—it was so easy and, it was, after all, the only way he knew how to speak. But even he could tell it wasn't helping. He'd joined the basketball team in hopes of reminding Adam of the good times they'd had together, thinking that the easy jock banter would help them gloss over the past. But Adam seemed to get angrier with every passing day—and, much as Kane hated to admit it to himself, the whole situation made him uncomfortable. He still didn't think he had any reason to feel guilty, but he'd feel much better if he could persuade Adam to feel the same way.

"What are you doing here?" Adam asked gruffly, breaking

into a run, dribbling the ball downcourt, away from Kane.

"Thought I might give you some help with your little problem," Kane called, running after him.

"What problem?" Adam bristled, shoving Kane away.

"Whatever you want to call it—'performance anxiety'?"

Adam suddenly tripped over the ball and fell flat on his ass. Kane tried hard—if not hard enough—not to laugh. Performance anxiety indeed.

"Who told you about that?" Adam asked hotly, standing up, grabbing the ball, and walking it back up court.

Kane slipped it out of his hands and began dribbling away.

"Everyone knows," he pointed out. "Or have you already forgotten that the whole town saw you choke the other night?"

"You're talking about basketball?" Adam asked, visibly relieved.

Kane launched the ball up for a perfect three-pointer and glanced over at Adam. "What did you think I was talking about?"

"Nothing," he muttered, chasing the ball out of bounds. "It doesn't matter. What do you want?"

"Like I said, I want to help." Kane had no trouble with fake sincerity—but the real kind always came out sounding forced. Mocking.

"I don't need your help. And you don't believe in it. So really, what do you want?"

Kane steeled himself. What he was about to do, he'd never done before—but how hard could it be, right? Other guys—lesser guys—did it all the time, and Kane knew he was as tough as any of them. "I just wanted to say—" He stopped, struggling to choke out the words. It was like Beth said: You had to close your eyes. And jump. "I'm sorry."

Adam whipped his head around. "You're *sorry*?" he said incredulously.

"Yeah." Kane grinned, proud of himself for making the effort—and Adam, of all people, should know exactly how much of an effort it had been. But he'd done it—and, you know? It hadn't been all that bad. "I'm sorry," he repeated, just because he could.

"Gosh, Kane, I've never heard you apologize before," Adam marveled. "That must have been really difficult for you."

"It wasn't all that bad, really. But, you know, our friendship's worth more than my stupid pride."

"Yeah, coming here, humbling yourself—that's real love," Adam said, and Kane suddenly gave him a closer look. Sarcasm was rare for Adam—and it showed. "I mean, you betray me, steal my girlfriend, humiliate me in front of the whole school, *destroy* me—but hey, you're sorry. Do you know how much that means to me?"

Kane said nothing.

"It means *shit*!" Adam yelled, hurling the ball toward Kane's head—who ducked just in time. "You think you can come here, say, 'I'm sorry, bro,' and I'm supposed to laugh it off? Now what—you, me, and Beth all go out and get drunk together? Like it's no big deal?"

"It doesn't have to be a big deal," Kane pointed out. "You're just making it into one. She's just a girl—"

"You *would* say that." Adam shook his head and jogged over to the side of the court to grab his T-shirt and his car keys, and began stalking toward the parking lot. "I'm sorry too," he called over his shoulder. "Sorry I was ever stupid enough to think we were friends. Sorry I ever let you into my life just so you could piss all over it. Guess what, Kane? Some mistakes you don't make twice."

Kane picked up the ball that Adam had left behind and slammed it angrily into the ground. Adam wanted to sulk, Adam wanted to hate him forever? Let him. Kane had violated his own policy, had opened himself up, put himself out there for someone else—and look how he'd been rewarded. He'd tried, he'd failed—and that was it.

Adam had at least been right about one thing, Kane thought: Some mistakes, you don't make twice.

"Can you believe it?" Adam asked, still fuming, hours after he'd left Kane on the basketball court.

Harper sat in the corner of his bedroom, knees hugged to her chest. She shook her head. "No, Ad, I can't believe it, any more than I could believe it the last ten times you told me the story."

Adam ignored the undercurrent of irritation in her voice—he was still too upset to give Harper's mood much thought. He'd called her as soon as he got home, needing some solace, a sympathetic ear—and whatever had, or hadn't, happened between them, she was always the person he turned to when he needed a friend. But here they were, sitting across the room from each other, this huge distance between them. And it was only making him feel worse.

"Like he could just say 'sorry' and I'd forgive him," Adam raged. "Like I could ever forgive him for what he did."

"I know. It was horrible," Harper said mechanically.

"Though at least he did apologize. You know what I can't get over? *Beth* has never apologized! Never even admitted what she did. I mean, if she could just accept some responsibility—"

"Adam!" Harper shouted suddenly. "Stop!"

"What?" He looked over at her, suddenly noticing her red-rimmed eyes, the lines of tension around her mouth. "What's wrong?"

"What's wrong is, I'm tired, and hung over, and sick of hearing this."

"Excuse me if I'm boring you," he said hotly. "I just thought—"

"Ad, I'm your best friend," Harper said, standing up. "And as your best friend, I'm happy to listen to anything you need to say. . . . But as your *girlfriend,* I can't listen to another word about how Kane and Beth broke your heart. If you want her back so bad, why don't you just go and get her? What the hell are you doing here with me?"

Adam hopped up and strode over to her, but she pushed him away.

"I know you're just with me as . . . a fallback," Harper said, her voice breaking. "Could you make it any more obvious? I can't be Beth for you, Adam," she cried, hitting at his chest as he tried to pull her into an embrace. "I tried . . . but I just can't."

"Who said I wanted you to be?" Adam asked quietly.

"You didn't have to say it. I'm not an idiot."

"Could have fooled me." He led her over to the edge of his bed. "Harper, sit down. Please. There's something I want to show you."

She sat down grudgingly, a scowl masking the tears

straining at the corners of her eyes. Adam opened the closet door and began digging through a pile of junk in the back—it had to be here somewhere. He would never have thrown it away. Finally, he found it—at the bottom of an old shoe box, tucked beneath a fraying stack of baseball cards and an old Lakers cap.

He turned back to Harper and placed it in her hands, sitting down on the bed beside her and putting an arm around her shoulders.

"What is this supposed to be?" Harper asked, holding the graying, chewed-leather leash between two fingers with a look of distaste. "If this is your way of telling me you need a girlfriend you can control, I already told you, I'm not Beth and—"

"Harper, just stop for a minute," Adam said, taking one end of the leash and running his hands across it. He'd forgotten the feel of the worn leather beneath his fingers, how comforting it could be.

"Did I ever tell you I used to have a dog?" he asked, closing his eyes for a moment to picture the scrappy terrier he'd had to leave behind. "We left Calvin in South Carolina when we moved." Adam could still see Calvin's droopy face, watching Adam walk out the door one last time, as if, somehow, he knew his owner was never coming back. His ears and tail stuck straight out at right angles, he hadn't barked, hadn't whimpered, hadn't run after the car—he'd just stood there and watched as Adam had abandoned him. His father had promised to look out for Calvin, but Adam knew that would never happen. And so he hadn't been surprised, a few months later, to get the call. It had been a big truck. Fast. Unavoidable. A painless way to go. So his father had said.

"When I moved here, I didn't know anyone," he continued, shaking off the memory. "Didn't have any friends, the house was this strange place, and my mother, well, you know . . ."

Harper didn't say anything, but she nodded, and her face had softened into a pensive frown.

"I brought this leash with me and, I guess I was so desperate for a friend that—" Adam paused. This was more embarrassing than he'd expected it to be. He looked over at Harper, semi-patiently waiting for him to get to the point. He'd keep going—she was worth it. "I pretended like Calvin was still here. I'd walk that leash all over town, talking to Calvin, telling him everything, how I hated my mother for bringing me here, how I was lonely, how I missed home and wanted to go back, even if—well, I told him everything. It sounds pretty ridiculous now," he admitted, blushing at the memory, "walking all over town, talking to myself. But I couldn't have made it here without him. Not at first."

Harper sighed and dropped her end of the leash. "It's a nice story, Ad, but I don't get it. Why haven't I ever heard about this before? And why tell me now? What's the point?"

"That *is* the point, Harper." He dropped the leash on the floor and put his arms around her. "You never heard about Calvin because, once I met you, I didn't need him anymore. I had something real I could count on. I put this leash away in a box and never looked at it again. I didn't need some imaginary friend to keep me from feeling lonely. When I met you, Harper, I knew I'd never be alone again."

"That's sweet, Ad, but—"

"No, not 'but'—you need to hear this, and you need to believe it." He'd never spoken to her, or anyone, this honestly before, had never even said these words in his own mind, but knew suddenly that they were true, and that this was something he should have said a long time ago. "You are the most important person in my life, Harper. Not Beth, *you*. I know it took me a while to figure things out—"

"A long while," she teased him, but she was finally smiling, though her eyes still shone with tears.

"But now I know, and I'm sure, it's always been you, Gracie. I don't want you to be like anyone else. I don't want you to change, or to doubt me. I just want you. I—" He'd only said this to one other girl in his life, and it had ended in disaster. He'd vowed to be more careful, to go slow, to guard himself against more pain. But he couldn't hold back. Not when it felt so right. "I think I love you, Harper."

"I love you, too, Adam," she whispered, and melted into him, her lips meeting his in a warm kiss. He laid her back against the bed, her wild hair splayed out against his pillows, and he thought idly that it was a good thing he'd changed his sheets the day before—and then the stray thought was knocked out of his head by an overwhelming rush of desire as she stripped off her shirt and he fell upon her perfect body. As he ran his fingers across her arms, her back, her chest, she wrapped herself around him.

It's happening, he thought in wonder. This time, it was really going to happen. It wasn't like with Kaia, the intoxication of passion mixed with guilt and bewilderment, or with Beth, a battle, a physical debate in which he always needed to prove himself worthy of her, and always failed to make his case. This was easy. This was right.

As he wriggled out of his jeans and groped in his nightstand for a condom, he felt a flash of panic—what if he failed once again? If he just wasn't capable?

But then, just as suddenly, the terror passed—and all it took was a look at her face, her eyes closed, the edges of her lips pulled into a blissed-out grin. This was Harper—and with the same warm certainty that all those years ago had allowed him to banish his imaginary friend, Adam relaxed. This was Harper—and nothing bad could ever happen to him with her by his side. Together, they could take on the world. Together, they made sense.

Together forever. It was the kind of promise children made to each other, he thought, before they knew anything about a world that could tear them apart. It was such a naive vision of the future—pure, innocent. And maybe that was okay, maybe that was right—because he and Harper had been children together for so long.

Today, together, it was finally time to grow up.

chapter

12

Have you been good this year?
Very, very good?
Too bad.
Reality check: Santa doesn't care if you're
naughty or nice. So you might as well have a
little fun. And there's still time.
New Year's Eve
512 Red Rock Road
9 p.m. to dawn
Start your New Year off right—or,
even better, very, very wrong.
—K

Adam locked the front door behind him and walked across the lawn to Harper's house. He put his finger on the doorbell, but stopped, suddenly, before pressing down.

In all the years he'd known her, Harper had never been

on time. She would never notice if he took a moment for himself, to think.

New Year's Eve—and look how things had ended up, he thought, sitting down on the front stoop. Last year at this time, he and Beth had driven out to an empty spot in the desert—the same place that, months before, they'd shared their first kiss. They'd huddled together on a blanket spread out across the uneven ground, their faces flickering in candlelight. He had never wanted anyone so much—and never been so sure of anything. He'd believed in Beth, believed she was the last girl, the only girl, he'd ever want to be with. He would have done anything for her, he'd realized that night.

She'd destroyed all that—and he had thought he would never move on. That things would never be the same.

And they weren't—they were better. Adam looked up at Harper's window, wondering what she was doing, what she was thinking. He was thinking about her, and only her—and about the way her body had felt against his. There was no one to clap Adam on the back, to tell him job well done, but he beamed with pride nonetheless— after all, he'd proven to himself, to the world, that he was a real man. Had taken Harper in his arms and shown her how he really felt. How much he needed her—and discovered how much she needed him.

All the pain, all the resentment, all the anger he'd carried around with him these last several weeks—he was done with it, he decided. A real man didn't need to hold a grudge. Didn't need closure, or revenge. He resolved that, this year, he would treat himself to a fresh start. He would truly, finally move on, whatever it took. He was big enough to move on—maybe even, with the new strength Harper had given him, big enough to forgive and forget.

Forget it, Kane told himself, again. Just forget. Move on. It's done.

But Adam's jeering face kept swimming back into focus in his mind's eye. Kane had exposed himself—and failed. And he didn't like it.

Winning came easy to Kane. But then, he usually chose his contests well. After all, any game you couldn't win wasn't worth the effort. That was his first rule: Pick your battles, and pick them wisely. His second? It's not over until *you* say it's over—and Beth was a case in point. Adam thought he'd won, had sat back and enjoyed his illusion of victory, and only Kane had understood that the game was still afoot. He'd bided his time; then, when the moment was just right, had played his hand. And he'd won in the end, as usual. As always.

And that was it, Kane had finally realized. Adam couldn't stand to lose. Too bad—who could? Was Kane supposed to restrain himself, refrain from pursuing his own desires, just because Adam wasn't able to protect his own turf?

Not a chance. And with that, Kane felt the annoying tendrils of guilt release their tight grip around his neck. He'd done what was needed to win. And since life itself was nothing more than competition, how could that be wrong? Kane based all his actions on cool logic, on strategy—and it always led to victory. Let your emotions get involved, and things just got messy. This episode with Adam was proof enough of that.

No more, Kane resolved, ducking into a convenience store to pick up a few essential items for the big party. (Noisemakers, confetti, and condoms—after all, hope springs eternal.) Emotional attachment and clear thinking didn't mix—and it was only by holding on to the latter that he could survive. Thrive.

As for Beth . . . he'd just have to be careful not to get too close. Kane had proven to himself, to her, to everyone, that he was the better man, that he could win her heart. Now he just needed to decide what he wanted to do with it.

What do you want? Beth asked herself, sitting down on the curb in front of her house, waiting for Kane to arrive. Better to wait outside, in the crisp, quiet night, than in the noisy, claustrophobic house, dodging nosy parents and sugar-crazed siblings. She needed her space. And time to think.

Last year, it had seemed like such an easy question. She wanted Adam. He wanted her. And for so long, they were happy.

The first words I heard this year were I love you, Beth thought in wonder. *From Adam.* He'd said it at midnight, and they'd greeted the New Year with a soft kiss that felt like it could last until spring. *Everything began with him.*

"I love you, too," she had whispered, believing it to be true. But maybe she'd been wrong. Maybe Adam had just been easy. Safe. She'd never worried about what he really wanted, or why he wanted her around. She'd just accepted him, and everything he said—and look what had happened.

So maybe, just maybe, she was better off. Adam had cast her aside—but had she crumbled? Had she given up? Not Beth. Never. She'd moved forward, moved past Adam, found herself a new guy, a new life. And Kane wasn't easy. He wasn't safe. Life with him was a risk, every day a new challenge.

For so long she'd questioned that, wondered if it was a sign that she'd made the wrong decisions, that her life had run off the tracks. But now? Beth meant everything she'd said in her essay—truly wanted to be that person, someone who took chances, someone who embraced the new, the different, the difficult. And she finally knew she was strong enough to do it.

She'd proven to herself that she could handle anything—and so, she resolved, this year she'd put aside her doubts and her fear. She'd try to loosen the reins a bit and embrace uncertainty. Maybe her life was headed off the track she'd set for herself—and maybe she didn't care.

I don't care what he thinks of me, Miranda told herself, over and over again. He was just a guy from the Internet—she didn't know him, might never see him again after tonight, so none of it really mattered. She had nothing to lose. So why was she short of breath, and so nervous she felt ready to pass out?

She hadn't eaten anything all day. Could you lose weight just by skipping lunch and dinner? she wondered. It was too late to worry about that now, and definitely too late to try on yet another outfit in a desperate search for one that didn't make her look frumpy. At any other party it wouldn't have mattered. How many parties had she spent hours preparing for meeting Mr. Right only to spend her night trapped between Mr. Wrong and the punch bowl? But this party was different. Because this time, she knew Mr. Right would be there—and he'd be waiting for her.

ReadItAndWeep had forgiven her for standing him up and had agreed to try again. They would meet at 11:30 on Kaia's back deck—and if things went well, Miranda might finally get her New Year's Eve midnight kiss.

Miranda had read dozens of self-help articles, all promising that confidence was the key to attracting a mate. Believe you look good, they claimed, and *he'll* believe it too. Take pride in yourself—and gain his undying respect and admiration.

This year, Miranda resolved, she was going to give it a try. Starting tonight.

I look great.

I am smart, funny, and fabulous.

Any guy would be lucky to have me.

The words rang empty in her ears, but she said them aloud, over and over again. Conviction through repetition. She hoped.

Every year on this night, with no one to turn to at the stroke of midnight, she vowed that *next* year would be different. Next year, she'd find the right person, someone who would live up to her standards—and, as an added bonus, notice that she was alive. Next year she wouldn't be alone.

This is the year, she told herself with gritty determination, every January first.

Maybe this year, she'd finally been right.

Everything was right with the world. Finally. Adam loved her—he *loved* her. Harper couldn't stop repeating the words to herself. She adored the way they sounded.

He loves me.

Tonight, they would be admired, envied, the center of attention—and why not? They were the perfect couple. Every girl at that party would wish she could take Harper's place. But none of them ever would. Adam had made that clear—and Harper finally believed him.

She wrapped the glittery purple scarf around her neck—brand-new purchase, courtesy of Mom and Dad, though they didn't know it—and applied one last layer of raspberry lip gloss. Adam was due any minute, and she was running late—it had taken her far too long to decide what to wear. But the perfect outfit was essential: Everyone who was anyone would be at Kaia's tonight. Harper had seen to that.

A last-minute party wasn't the easiest thing to pull off, but Harper had plenty of connections—and, fortunately, the town of Grace wasn't about to offer much competition when it came to exciting nightlife. Even on New Year's Eve.

Harper had been happy to help. These days, she was happy to do pretty much anything. Being in love could do that to you. And not only was she happier than she'd ever been, but for the first time, it was a happiness that didn't depend on seeing others miserable.

Not completely, at least.

She slid on a pair of strappy silver heels that went perfectly with her silvery halter top, and checked herself out in the mirror.

I look hot, she thought approvingly. *I look like the kind of girl who* should *be dating the hottest guy in town.*

Officially, it was Kaia's party, she supposed. But it would be *Harper's* night. And, in a few more hours, the beginning of *Harper's* year. She'd wasted so much time worrying that Adam didn't want her, worrying that she should be a better person—screw that. Adam loved her just the way she was. He'd proven that much last night. And then again this afternoon. And Harper had proven to herself that she was every bit as incredible as she'd always thought.

It was New Year's Eve, a time for resolutions, and this year, Harper had only one: No more second-guessing herself, no more feeling guilty about how she might have acted, regretful about what she might have done. She deserved everything she had—and she had it all.

They say you can't have it all. But what did they know?

And what better way to celebrate her good fortune, Kaia decided, than to open her house to the peons and show off her remarkable house and her remarkable life?

She'd slipped into a dusty rose Miu Miu top, with deliciously expensive fabric and a plunging neckline, and paired it with a suede skirt she'd picked up at a Betsey Johnson sample sale last year. The color looked fabulous against her deep tan—which, she had to admit, was even better than the one she'd picked up last winter break, sipping Margaritas on a yacht off the coast of Turks and Caicos.

Too bad that, along with her perfect wardrobe and her perfect tan, she couldn't show off her perfect man. Jack Powell was considered such a prize—Grace's bachelor #1— it was a shame Kaia couldn't broadcast their relationship to the world. Powell had his choice of any girl, any woman he wanted—and he wanted Kaia.

To think she'd almost let herself get distracted, by Reed, of all people. Pizza boy had something, that was clear. But it wasn't anything she wanted. Not while she had a man like Jack Powell at her beck and call. Living in New York City had taught Kaia a few things, and she knew that you didn't trade in your penthouse for a tenement. First-class apartments were hard to come by—almost as hard as first-class guys. *Especially* in a place like this.

Kaia and Jack Powell, together? That was a power couple, a pair who would turn heads.

Kaia and Reed Whoever? An image like that could only turn stomachs—starting with Kaia's own.

So what if she found Reed intriguing, if her heart pounded a little faster, a little louder when he was around? All that was in the past—and, she resolved, it was going to stay that way. The New Year meant no more Reed. No more playing with fire—and no more digging through the trash.

Kaia was strict about her New Year's resolutions, stricter than most—she usually lasted well into February.

This year, she lasted about five minutes. And then the doorbell rang.

She checked her watch—8:30—still far too early for even the most overeager of guests. And Kaia was pretty sure Harper wouldn't have invited anyone clueless enough to even show up on time. Or did they not do fashionably late out here in hicksville?

She opened the door—and there he was, the same ratty T-shirt, the same smoldering eyes, and suddenly she was right back where she'd started.

On the brink of disaster.

"I heard you're having a party," Reed said by way of greeting. "My invitation must have gotten lost in the mail."

"You weren't—" Kaia cut herself off, torn between wanting to slam the door in his face and wanting to rip his clothes off. Telling him he purposely hadn't been invited didn't seem like the right move, but what if he wanted to stay? *That* could never be allowed. Your guest list defined you, and she refused to be known as the type of girl who invited—or even acknowledged the existence of—his type of guy.

"I don't do parties," he informed her.

She struggled not to look too relieved. On the other hand, she wasn't quite ready for him to leave. And she definitely wasn't ready for the realization that a part of her wanted to leave with him. "So why are you here?" she asked, trying to sound as if she didn't care.

Which, she assured herself, she didn't.

"I figured we'd start the New Year together," he explained.

"It's eight thirty," she pointed out caustically.

"I thought you could just pretend," he said, flashing a knowing grin. "You're good at that."

He pulled out a paper noisemaker and gave it a half-hearted toot. Then, tossing it aside, he pulled her into his arms.

"Happy New Year," he whispered, his breath hot against her cheek, and then kissed her, sucking deeply on her lower lip, digging his hands into her flesh. She tore at him with urgency, at first, and then something shifted—the rough and raw energy between them softened, deepened.

As his hands cupped her face, she opened her eyes, and he was watching her, his bottomless brown eyes only centimeters away. She could see herself reflected in them. She closed her eyes again and shut in the darkness, her world narrowed to the taste of his lips, the touch of his fingers, the sound of his breathing.

Happy New Year? She mused. *Just maybe.*

chapter

13

"You're the only one I want, the only one I need. . . ."

Adam let the lyrics wash over him and pulled Harper in tighter as they swayed slowly back and forth to the music. She leaned her head on his shoulder, her auburn waves cascading down his chest.

Kaia's house, even more impressive than he'd remembered, was filled with people—some lounging in the hot tub, some picking their way through the gourmet spread, and a few couples off on the fringes, lost in their own world, like Harper and Adam.

A cool, bluish light lit the oversize room, giving the stark white furniture and walls an icy sheen.

"I could never live here," Harper murmured, voicing his thoughts. "It's too . . ."

"Cold," he finished for her. And it was true. Living like this, like Kaia, you could freeze to death.

"But it's a great party," she continued. "Don't you think?"

"Definitely." Also true. "But any party would be great—

with you." Adam had already had a couple drinks, and, with a little alcohol poured into him, his cheesiness factor sky-rocketed.

Harper raised her head from his shoulder and looked him in the eye. "Ad, you don't need to butter me up. You've already got me," she pointed out, giving him a quick kiss on the cheek.

"What?" he asked defensively. "It's true!"

She laughed and shook her head, her hair whipping across his face. "You're a little drunk, my friend. But you're also pretty damn sweet, so I guess it's okay."

"Well, as long as I have your permission," he blustered.

She laid her head back against his shoulder. "I love this song," she said softly.

"All I ever needed, here in your arms . . ."

More couples had joined them on the impromptu dance floor—but only one of them caught Adam's eye.

Kane had his back turned, but Adam could see her face, peeking over Kane's shoulder. Her blond hair was down, falling across her cheek like a golden curtain. And her clear blue eyes met his.

". . . the only one I want, the only one I need . . ."

He closed his eyes—but he still saw her face.

Beth jerked her head away.

Stop watching him, she instructed herself sternly, know-ing it was no use. She'd been following him with her eyes all night, catching a glimpse of him embracing Harper by the doorway, holding hands on the stairs, kissing on the back deck. They were everywhere—and Beth couldn't force herself to stay away.

"What's wrong?" Kane asked, peering down at her in concern.

"Nothing," she said quietly, thinking fast. "I was just looking . . . at all these couples dancing. It's kind of sad, isn't it, how no one really dances anymore?"

"We're dancing," he pointed out.

"No, that's not what I mean. We're just standing in one place, rocking back and forth. That's not dancing—not *really*. In the old days . . ."

"Let me guess: women in fancy ball gowns, men in tuxedos sweeping them around the dance floor?" he suggested.

"Waltzing the night away," she added, with a dreamy, faraway smile.

"Don't forget the 'forbidden dance,'" he put in with a smirk.

She gave him a teasing push. "Kane, I'm serious!"

"And like I always say, your wish is my command." He grabbed her hand in his, placing her other hand firmly at his waist. "Let's go."

"Go where—?"

Without answering, he swept her feet off the floor and, in classic ballroom form, began leading her around the room, weaving through couples and crowds of people, twirling her out and then reeling her back in.

"People are staring at us!" she gasped through her laughter.

"Let them stare," he crowed. "They're just jealous."

The whole room had, indeed, gradually stopped talking and turned to gape at the couple whirling through the room as if clumsy extras in a remake of *Cinderella*. But for once, Beth didn't care. She was having too much fun, breathless with laughter, flying in Kane's arms, feeling suddenly, wildly alive. He was right: Who cared what anyone thought?

Finally the song ended, and he dipped her with an exaggerated flourish and then swept her back up into a deep kiss. "Happy New Year," he whispered.

"I've never—that was unbelievable," she babbled, still flushed and giggling.

"I promised you I'd show you a good time," he reminded her. "You just have to trust me."

"I guess I've learned my lesson," she agreed, unable to stop smiling. She kissed him again. "So, what's next on the agenda?"

"Funny you should ask." He pulled a small box out of his pocket and handed it to her. "I've got a little surprise for you—Merry belated Christmas."

"What is it?" she asked in delight, tearing off the wrapping paper. Her smile faded as she opened the box and saw what lay inside.

Two small yellow tablets. And that was it.

"Kane, what is this?" she asked in a dull, flat voice.

"Just something to make our New Year's *ex*tra special," he explained, putting an arm around her.

She shrugged it off.

"I don't do drugs," she snapped. "You know that."

"It's not like this would make you a junkie," he wheedled. "It's just something special, a one-time deal. And you won't *believe* how it will make you feel."

Beth suddenly felt like she was in the middle of one of those horrible after-school specials they forced on you in junior high health class, where the heroine almost bows to peer pressure but, in the end, wises up and decides to "just say no!" Or maybe this was one of those where the heroine decides to throw caution to the wind . . . and ends up living in a cardboard box with needle tracks tracing across her arms.

No, I don't do drugs, she'd assured her parents the one time they'd gotten up the nerve to ask. *Trust me, even if I wanted to, I wouldn't know where to find them.*

It had been true—for seventeen years—and now, suddenly, it wasn't.

Beth looked at the small open box, the innocuous-looking tablets. How much harm could they do, just this one time? What about all her talk about trying new things, taking risks—was it just that? Talk? She was always so predictable, so *good,* always doing the right thing. She looked across the room and there he was again, Adam—her gaze drawn to him no matter how hard she tried to avoid it. He kissed Harper, and Beth shivered. She'd done the right thing with him, and where had it gotten her? He still thought she was a cheater. A traitor. Everyone did. So why not actually *do* something, for once? It's not like she had a reputation to protect, not anymore. Was she going to go through her life too afraid of consequences to ever really *live?*

She picked up one of the pills between her thumb and index finger and looked at it thoughtfully.

"You said you wanted some excitement in your life, a thrill," Kane pointed out. "This is it—it's like nothing you've ever felt before."

"I don't know, Kane . . . it's not . . . is it safe?"

"As safe as can be," he promised. "Would I be willing to take them myself if it weren't safe?"

She raised an eyebrow, and he gave her a rueful grin.

"You have a point," he admitted. "But I would never put you in danger." He grabbed her and kissed her, lifting her off the ground, and then, slowly, eased her back down to earth. "I just want to show you something that's almost as amazing as you are."

It was tempting—and it would be so easy to say yes. But skiing down a mountain was one thing, Beth decided. Throwing yourself off a cliff was another. "I don't think so," she said, wishing she sounded more resolute.

"Come on," Kane urged. "You know you want to."

Beth looked at him and, suddenly, snapped back to reality. *You know you want to?* This wasn't even *creative* peer pressure—it was absurdly textbook, as if he'd lifted the line from a drug pusher's manual: *How to Drug Friends and Influence People.* She might be naive, but not naive enough to fall for this.

Beth put the tablet back into the box, replaced the lid, and tried to hand it back to Kane, but he refused.

"Take it," he said irritably. "I went to a lot of trouble to get these. I promise nothing will happen to you. Don't you want to have some fun, for once in your life?"

Without a word, she slipped the box into her purse, shook her head, and began to turn away. She needed—well, she didn't know what she needed, exactly, other than to be somewhere else, away.

"Don't you trust me?" he asked plaintively.

And that's when she finally figured it out.

No. I don't.

It was 11:29, and Miranda pushed her way out to the back deck, her heart pounding in her chest. He was out there, somewhere, her mystery man. He'd told her he would be wearing a gray-and-green-striped shirt, and she'd told him she would be wearing a pale blue, off-the-shoulder top. She still hadn't told him that she was mousy and flat-chested, with rust-colored hair and a big mouth—but he'd find all that out soon enough. She hoped he wouldn't care.

She saw the shirt first.

Normal build, normal height, no extra limbs—so far, so good.

Then she saw his face.

She raised her eyes to the ceiling. Was it too much to ask that she not be the punch line of *every* cosmic joke?

Introducing Bachelor #1: Greg. Of course. The Greg she'd dated a couple of times and then blown off, the Greg who reamed her out every time he saw her, then raced off in the opposite direction. Miranda choked back a spurt of crazed laughter and resisted the impulse to offer up a feeble request: Can I see what's behind door number two?

But then, maybe because of the champagne, maybe because of the holiday spirit, maybe because she was just tired of being alone, Miranda took a moment. And reconsidered. After all, she remembered another Greg, the one who had been so good to her, before everything went down. A guy it had been so easy for her to talk to, and who, back in the beginning, at least, had seemed to like her so much.

Maybe this wasn't such a disaster. Maybe it was actually the universe's way of giving her a second chance.

"Miranda?" he asked in disbelief. "Please tell me *you're* not Spitfire?"

"Guilty," she replied with a weak smile.

The look on his face mirrored her own expression of a moment before: a mixture of disappointment, incredulity, and disgust.

"It figures," he mumbled under his breath, and turned to walk away.

"Greg, wait," Miranda said, grabbing his arm. "I know this seems—"

"Pathetic? Like a cruel joke?"

"Weird," she said firmly. "But think about it. This kind of makes sense. We have a lot in common, we get along . . . we used to get along. . . . Maybe this is a sign? That we should give it another shot?"

"A sign?" He shot her a look of disbelief, then shook his head. "It's a sign, all right—a sign that I should have listened to my instincts, that I should have known better than to try to meet someone on a Web site. What was I thinking—what kind of girl could I really have expected to find on the *Internet*?"

"Could you lower your voice?" Miranda begged, edging away from him as the people nearby turned to stare.

"I told myself they wouldn't all be desperate and pathetic," he continued, just as loudly. "I lied to myself. I should have known, they would all be just like *you*."

Kane took another gulp of vodka from his trusty silver flask.

She'd walked away from him. Again. On New Year's.

This was getting old.

And what had he done wrong this time? Just tried to show her how to have a little fun. But she was too good for that, wasn't she? Too trapped by her narrow-minded view of the world to even notice when someone offered her an escape route.

Kane reached in his pocket and pulled out another of the little yellow pills. Good thing he'd kept an extra supply on hand, just in case. He had hoped they could share this experience, that it would loosen her up and bring them closer—and isn't that what she was always whining about? Wishing he would open up, let her get close? She'd had her chance—and she'd blown it.

He popped the pill in his mouth and let it dissolve on his tongue, washing it down with another swig of vodka.

He hated to take this stuff on his own, it was such a waste—but soon the drug would sweep over him and take him away, and then he wouldn't care. Besides, he was used to alone. Alone was how he lived. It had never stopped him before, and it wouldn't stop him tonight.

He wouldn't let it.

She'd been a fool. Made an enormous mistake. That much was clear. But so much was still muddy and confusing.

Beth threaded her way through the crowd and found her way out to the back deck, taking a deep gulp of fresh air. Turning her back on the noise of the party and the revelers in the hot tub, she leaned against the railing and looked out into the night. She'd made a mistake, yes. But what was it? Walking away from Kane? Or walking toward him in the first place?

Half of her wanted to run back into the party and

apologize; the other half wanted to leave and never look back. And, much as she hated to admit it, there was a small, small part of her conscious of the pills lodged in her purse, wondering: What if . . . ?

Too many options; too many decisions. So instead, she stayed at the railing, still, willing herself to think about something other than herself, than her bad choices. If she could clear her mind completely, maybe she could start over, start fresh. But before she could reboot, she'd need to shut down her mind, shut off her thoughts—and they were racing too quickly to be caught.

She heard the footsteps, getting closer and closer, then stop, just behind her.

She heard her name spoken, softly, hesitantly.

But she didn't turn around—not yet. She didn't know what she was going to say. And as long as she kept her back to him, she wouldn't have to decide.

"How many rooms does this place have?" Harper asked in astonishment as she stumbled into the study after Kaia.

"I'm still trying to figure that out," Kaia giggled.

Harper goggled at the room as they stepped inside—it was about eight by eight and, as far as she could tell, seemed to serve mainly as a closet for the Sellers' CDs. "This is unbelievable," she gushed.

Under normal circumstances she might not have been so eager to expose her awe at Kaia's starring role in *Lifestyles of the Rich and Bitchy*, preferring to mask her longing for the other girl's clothes, car, house . . . life. But these weren't normal circumstances. It was New Year's Eve, she was at a party, her life was nearly perfect—and she'd already had maybe a little too much of the fluorescent pink punch sitting in a Waterford crystal bowl by the door of the kitchen. She was totally buzzed—but was it the alcohol? she wondered. Or was it Adam?

Kaia, a few miles away from sober herself, was pawing frantically through the wall of CDs. "I know it's in here somewhere," she insisted. "You have got to hear this song."

"I can hear it later," Harper pointed out. "We can't spend the whole night in here while you look." But she wasn't annoyed—her umbrella of goodwill was large enough to cover Kaia. Especially since Kaia was, after all, the one who'd delivered Adam to her doorstep. She felt a wave of friendship toward her former rival and, just as Kaia found the right CD and slipped it into the stereo, pulled her into the center of the room, and began twirling her around. An intense driving beat burst from the speakers, matched by a pumping base line. Harper and Kaia whirled around, throwing themselves into the music, the moment.

Suddenly, the door swung open, and Kane stumbled into the room, grabbing Harper away from Kaia and swinging her into his arms. "Can I cut in?" he asked gruffly and belatedly, his breath hot and stinking of vodka.

Harper pushed him away. "Get off, Kane. You're drunk," she complained in disgust.

"Oh, and you're not?" he countered, grabbing her again and trying to kiss her.

She veered away, and his lips smeared across her cheek. She'd never seen him like this—so *sloppy*. Beneath his lackadaisical front, Harper knew, lay a total control freak—and yet, at the moment, he was most definitely out of control.

"What's the matter, you don't think I'm sexy?" he slurred, flexing a bicep.

"Yeah, Kane, you're really sexy," she agreed sarcastically. "Especially now."

"Oh, I'm not good enough for you now?" he asked hostilely, lurching backward.

"Why do you care?" she snapped. "You're with Beth now, *remember*? Where is she, anyway?" Harper looked around in mock confusion. "Having a little trouble keeping track of your date?"

"Apparently no more than you are," he shot back, his voice suddenly clear and steady. "Or has Adam's personality finally faded so much that he's turned invisible?"

Harper ignored the insult and immediately poked her head out into the main party area, ready to prove Kane wrong.

But Adam was nowhere to be seen.

And neither was Beth.

"Lose something?" Kane asked sardonically.

She barely heard him—she was too busy asking herself the same question.

chapter

14

He found Beth out on the deck, her back to the party, staring aimlessly out at the dark desert expanse stretching beneath her.

"Beth?" he said quietly—no answer.

Tentatively, he touched her shoulder, and she whirled around. But her face relaxed as soon as she recognized him.

"Oh, it's just you." She sighed.

"Are you okay out here?" he asked, noticing that her eyes were red and glassy with unshed tears.

"I'm fine," she assured him. "Just . . . thinking."

"Yeah, I've been doing a lot of that lately," he commiserated, leaning up against the rail that encircled the deck. "And there's something I want to talk to you about."

She ran a weary hand through her hair.

"Adam, I don't really have the energy right now for—"

"Then just listen," he begged her. "I need to say this. It's New Year's, you know."

"Yes, I'd noticed," she said dryly.

"I don't want to start the new year like this," he told her. With us—like this."

She wrinkled her face in confusion. "Are you saying you want us to get back—"

"No, no, no," he cut her off hastily. Was that relief in her eyes? Or disappointment? "No—I just hate it that we can't even talk anymore." *Except for that afternoon in the mountains,* he didn't say, though he wanted to. *That day when it seemed like things could be . . . different. Better.*

"We're talking now," she pointed out.

Just be direct, he coached himself. Beth had hurt him, badly—but he had to let it go. He couldn't move on if he was still trying to punish her, he'd realized. And also . . . he just couldn't stand to hurt her anymore. No matter what she'd done to him.

"I want to apologize," he finally blurted out. "I've treated you like shit. I've been horrible to you, and I realize now I was wrong."

"Well, that's nice of you, but . . ."

"We all make mistakes, Beth," he pressed on, "and I should never have expected you to be perfect. So I want you to know"—he took a deep breath, for this was an incredibly difficult sentiment for him to express—"I forgive you."

"You forgive me?" she asked incredulously. "*You* forgive *me*?"

He'd expected tears of gratitude, an outpouring of shame, or even just a wordless hug—but he hadn't been prepared for the wave of anger flooding her face.

"You forgive me for what?" she snapped.

She had to ask?

"You know for what—for *Kane,*" he hissed.

"How many times do I have to tell you that nothing *happened?*" she cried.

Adam felt his muscles clench and he tried to stay calm. He couldn't believe it. He'd worked so hard to do the mature thing, swallow his pride, offer his forgiveness—and she still couldn't even admit what she'd done to him?

"You can tell me as many times as you want," he retorted, his voice rising, "but it won't help. I know what you did. Why can't you just admit it?"

"There's nothing to admit!" she exclaimed.

"I can't—" He started to turn away, then stopped. He couldn't keep doing this to himself. He couldn't start the year off like this. It wasn't fair—to anyone. "Look, I didn't come out here to start a fight with you," he said softly, turning back around.

"I don't want to fight anymore either," she admitted, the tension visibly leaching out of her body.

"Can we call a truce?" he asked hopefully. "Agree to disagree?"

She nodded. "I'd like that."

They stood facing each other in silence for a moment, and then Adam broke the wall of distance with a hug, sweeping her into his arms. Her hair still smelled like lilacs, fresh and sweet. It felt so right to hold her, to remember the way her body had fit snugly against his. And she clung to him, her arms wrapped tightly around his neck, her face buried in his shoulder, and he could feel her crying—but when she finally looked up at him, her eyes were dry.

"Remember last New Year's?" she asked, her arms still wrapped loosely around him, his arms lightly encircling her waist. When Adam was with Harper, pushing Beth out of his mind seemed so easy. But now, facing her, holding her, the past seemed more real than the present.

He nodded ruefully. "This isn't the way I thought things would end up."

She sighed. "I know. I guess I thought we would . . ."

"So did I," he said softly, brushing a tear from her cheek. Her skin was like silk. It would be so easy to lean forward just a bit, to close his eyes and forget where he was and what had happened between them, just to feel the tender touch of her lips again. He caught his breath for a moment, and all he could see were her lips, glossy and slightly parted, and all he could feel was his desperate need—

"We should really get back inside," she said awkwardly, breaking away from him.

He dropped his hands to his sides abruptly. What the hell had he been thinking?

"I should—go find Harper," he stammered.

"And Kane." She sighed. "I guess I should . . ." She shook her head. "Let's just go back inside." They threaded their way back toward the sliding-glass door to the living room, but before they stepped through, Adam stopped her.

"I'm glad we talked," he told her, leaning close. "I really want things to be better between us."

"They will," she promised, and took his hand.

They stood at the threshold, and Adam knew he had to step inside, rejoin the party, find Harper. But Beth's hand was still tightly wrapped around his, comforting and warm.

And he really didn't want to let go.

"I can't believe you let him out of your sight," Kane taunted her. "You really think that's safe?"

"Would you just shut up?" Harper snapped irritably. She was so sick of Kane's overblown ego, his superiority complex—as if he were really so much better than the rest of them. "Adam loves me," she maintained. "*I've* got nothing to worry about. You, on the other hand . . ."

She turned away to join Kaia, who was lying low and flipping through CDs in the back corner, obviously trying to stay out of the line of fire, but too curious to slip out of the room.

"And what's that supposed to mean?" Kane asked, flinging himself onto a small leather couch pressed against the wall. "Beth and I are just fine."

Harper just snorted.

"Got something you want to share with the rest of the class, Grace?"

"You and Beth are a walking disaster," she informed him. "A ticking time bomb, a train wreck, a—oh, pick whatever tired cliché you want. The whole relationship is a joke."

"I'm not laughing," he said in a dangerous voice.

"But everyone else is," Harper countered. "It's so obvious she'd never be with you if Adam hadn't broken up with her. She never would have even looked at you."

"What about you?" Kane asked, rising from the sofa and striding toward her. "Like Adam would ever have dropped Beth for the town *slut*?"

"You can insult me all you want," Harper said, feeling the bile rise in her throat. Sticks and stones may break your bones—but names seeped inside and killed you slowly from within. Not that she'd ever admit it. "But I know the truth," she insisted. "Adam *wants* to be with me."

"Only because he thinks Beth cheated on him," Kane pointed out.

"So?"

"*So?* So she *didn't*—or have you forgotten that little detail? In this delusional world you've created for yourself, have you forgotten that we just made him *think* she cheated on him?" He grabbed Harper by the shoulders and gave her a rough shake. "Snap out of it. He's not with you because he wants to be. He's with you because you tricked him. You lied to him."

"*We* lied," Harper corrected him. "And it doesn't matter." She pulled herself away and turned her back on him, hugging herself in an effort to hold it together. "He would have come to me eventually. We just sped things up a little."

"No, *Beth* would have come to *me* eventually," Kane countered. "They always do. You, on the other hand, would still be alone."

"Why are you doing this to me?" Harper asked in a tight and muffled voice.

"Why are *you* trying to pretend you're so much better than me, that your relationship with Adam is oh-so-perfect, while Beth and I are—" He turned Harper around to face him, and she met his gaze fiercely. "We're the same, you and I."

"We are *not*," she insisted.

She glared at Kane, at his smug, superior face. He didn't care about anyone, about whom he lied to, whom he hurt. That wasn't her, she assured herself. She only did what she did because she had to. It wasn't her fault. That person, cold and calculating, heartless—she could act the part, but it wasn't real. It wasn't *her*.

"We are, Harper," he pressed on. "Looking at you, it's like looking in a mirror. Why don't you just admit it? For once in your life, why don't you just tell the truth?"

"She doesn't know how."

Kane glanced up at the sound of the cold, thin voice— but Harper didn't need to. She'd recognized it. She'd know his voice anywhere. But finally she couldn't stand it anymore. She had to turn around, had to see his face—and Adam was frozen in the doorway, Beth by his side.

The world went dark for a moment, and Harper thought she would pass out—longed for unconsciousness. But then everything swam back into focus, and it was real. He was there. And from the look on his face, she could tell.

He'd heard everything.

At first, their angry voices hadn't really registered. Adam hadn't processed what they were saying, what it meant. It was only when Beth, standing beside him just outside the doorway of the small study, issued a quiet moan, that he had understood.

He had blundered in here looking for Harper, and he'd found her, he realized. The *real* Harper.

The four of them stood frozen in silence for a moment, just staring at one another in disbelief. Beth broke first.

"How could you?" she cried, her eyes whipping back and forth from Harper to Kane. "Did you really think you'd get away with this?"

Kane shrugged his shoulders and flopped down on the

couch. "Sure, I did," he admitted, his hands propped casually behind his head. "Don't tell me you're surprised."

"I-I-" Beth stopped stuttering and burst into tears, fleeing the room. Adam wanted to chase after her, but it was as if his feet were stuck to the floor. He couldn't move—couldn't take his eyes off Harper.

"Adam—" She rushed up to him, put her hands on his shoulders, "Adam, please, you have to understand."

Gently but firmly, he took her hands off his body and returned them to her sides.

"Don't touch me," he warned her in a low monotone. He felt a dull, hard anger spreading over his body. Not the burning rage that had swept over him when he'd found out about Beth. This was something different, something new. He felt calm and cold, as if his veins had turned to ice, as if something inside of him had died.

"You were my oldest friend, my best friend," he told her slowly. "I trusted you." Past tense. "I thought I *loved* you."

"Adam, please," Harper begged, tears streaming down her face. In all the years he'd known her, he had never seen her cry. He wondered idly whether he should be feeling surprise, or pity. He felt—nothing. Hollow. Spent.

"I love you, Adam!" Harper cried, throwing herself against his chest, clinging to him. "You mean everything to me."

"And you mean nothing to me," he spit out, pulling himself away. *"You're nothing."*

She flinched at his words, but he had moved beyond caring. He wasn't even trying to hurt her. He was just stating a truth. Everything he'd believed in, everything he'd trusted in, it had disappeared. There was nothing left but emptiness. The Harper he had known—the Harper he may have loved—just didn't exist. Smoke and mirrors, a pretty illusion. That was all.

"I have to go now," he said mechanically. "I have to find Beth."

"Then go," Harper said, slumping down to her knees as if she'd lost the strength to stand. "Just go. But you know you won't be happy with her, Adam. You know it won't be like what we had. What we had was real."

"And you killed it." Adam pointed out. "Maybe you can forgive yourself for that," he added, stepping around her and out the door, "but I can't."

chapter

15

Beth needed to get out, to get away. She felt like the walls were closing in on her, as if everyone were staring at her—the clamor of the party rose in her ears and hammered at her, crushing her. She just needed to go, to think.

She slipped out the front door and then paused, drawing in deep and desperate breaths of the dry night air. She supposed she should be worried about finding a way to get home, but that seemed like a remote problem, something that would take care of itself, somehow, sometime. Right now she just breathed in the peace and quiet, and waited.

Because deep down, she knew he would come.

And he did.

"I thought I'd find you out here," he said from behind her.

Beth didn't turn around.

Adam touched her back for an instant and then pulled his hand away.

"I don't know what to say," he admitted.

Beth hugged her arms to her chest. She could think of plenty of things for him to say: how he should have trusted her instead of throwing her away; how stupid he'd been to be duped by Harper's sadistic game . . . but then, hadn't she been just as stupid? Hadn't she fallen blindly into Kane's arms? Or worse, not so blindly. She'd seen what he was, she'd known it deep down, and she'd ignored it. She'd wanted so badly for it to work, for Kane to be the guy she needed him to be—for her new relationship to somehow *best* Adam's. It had all been more important to her than the truth.

She turned to face Adam, and almost gasped. He looked wrecked. Literally, as if a sudden storm had swept through his life and cast him on a barren shore. His eyes were hooded, his shoulders slumped.

"I—I'm sorry," he said, raising his hands from his sides, palms up in supplication. "I don't know what I'm supposed to do."

"You should never have trusted her word over mine," Beth pointed out.

Adam shook his head.

"No. But . . ." He looked up at her, his eyes welling with tears. "She was my best friend."

It was a sentiment Beth would be happy never to hear again, even in the past tense.

"And I was your girlfriend," she retorted angrily. "Why was it so hard for you to remember that part? *I* loved you too. *I* was always there for you—how could you think I could ever do anything like that?"

"I don't know!" he cried, his mouth twisting into a gash of pain. "I don't know."

He looked so miserable, so lonely, so bereft, she couldn't stand it.

"It's not all your fault," she offered, a note of sympathy entering her voice. "They played you. They played us both. How were you supposed to know?"

"I should have—" His voice faltered, and she took a few steps toward him, put her hands lightly on his shoulders.

"You should have trusted me," she said firmly. "But you didn't."

"Because I'm an idiot."

"Because something was wrong between us, Adam," she reminded him softly. "That's why you believed them. Because you and I, we were already—"

"Don't say that," he protested. "Please. I . . ." He closed his eyes for a moment. "I loved you. And you . . . I thought . . ."

"I loved you, too." It still hurt to say the words.

He tensed beneath her fingers.

"I still can't believe it," he said, his voice tight with anger. "How could anyone be so—" he choked himself off, shaking with rage.

"Adam, forget it," she advised him.

"Forget it?" he repeated incredulously. "And how the hell am I supposed to do that?"

"You just do." She turned him around to face her. "It was horrible, what they did," she agreed, shivering at the memory of Kane's arms cradling her as she cried and cried, and all the while, he'd been the cause of all her pain. "It was unspeakable, but in the end, they didn't get away with it," she pointed out. "We're here, now, together. Maybe this is . . ." She hesitated. "A second chance."

He grabbed her hands and pulled them to his chest. "You mean . . . ?"

"We've both done some things we regret," Beth told him. And it was true. She had shut him out, long before Kane and Harper broke into their lives. She'd stopped trusting him, picked fights over nothing. Harper and Kane had shoved them over a cliff—but they'd made it to the edge all by themselves. Maybe this was their do-over. "But maybe if we start off slow, forget the past . . . that is, if you still want to."

He brought her hands to his mouth and kissed them softly. "More than anything." He suddenly looked at his watch. "It's midnight," he told her with surprise. "Happy New Year."

She looked up at him and smiled. "I think it will be."

And then he kissed her.

"Happy New Year!" the roomful of drunken revelers shouted, throwing confetti and flinging themselves into one another's arms.

Miranda spotted Greg across the room, making out with some random girl. She couldn't pull her eyes away from them, Greg's hands running through her hair, their bodies wound together. That used to be her—could have been her.

She had hated kissing Greg, she reminded herself. It had been a total drag, long and wet and boring.

But standing there alone on yet another New Year's Eve, watching all these couples start off their year together, she wondered: Maybe her standards were too high, unrealistic. Maybe settling was better than being alone.

"There you are, Stevens!"

Miranda whirled around to see Kane, a wide grin stretched across his face, lurching toward her. He flung his arms around her and whirled her off the ground, and then, before she knew what was happening, gave her a wet and sloppy kiss. On the lips.

He had kissed her.

Kane's lips had just touched hers.

"Happy New Year!" he shouted, slinging an arm around her shoulders. Miranda barely heard him.

He'd kissed her.

And now, she was standing there, nestled beneath his arm, leaning against him, breathing in his familiar cologne.

He was obviously drunk or high—maybe both—it was the only time he ever showed any genuine affection to anyone. But Miranda didn't care. The alcohol, the drugs, whatever, they'd just loosened him up, cracked through that impenetrable veneer and dragged his real feelings to the surface.

He'd come to find her, at midnight—he'd kissed her. Not Beth, not any of his double-D ditzes. Her.

So he was drunk. So it had probably been a "just friends" kiss. So what? She was starting out the new year in Kane Geary's arms, and whatever happened next, she would always have this moment, this night.

And for right now, that was enough.

Harper watched Kane and Miranda celebrate together and smiled sadly. Miranda would be so pathetically happy at even the tiny, drunken show of affection. The next day she'd call Harper and they would spend hours dissecting the single moment. And the day after that? When she found out, as she inevitably would, that Harper had betrayed her, had pushed her "one true love" into the arms of their worst enemy?

Then she'd be gone from Harper's life, just like everyone else.

She'd just lost Miranda, even if Miranda didn't know it yet. But she couldn't muster up the strength to care. How could she focus on a trivial pain like that when her entire body, her whole being, was throbbing with the agony of having lost Adam? When he'd turned his back on her and walked away, she'd felt like a piece of herself had died.

If he'd only gotten angry. If he'd yelled, screamed, kicked something—anything but that cold, dead voice, those empty eyes. As if anything that had ever been between them was just—gone.

Her life was in ruins. Reduced to rubble.

Harper stood in the middle of the party, the crowd surging around her. She didn't cry. She didn't scream or tear at her hair or fall to the floor or do anything that might betray the searing pain within, that might show the world she'd been torn in two.

That wasn't her way—and, after all, what would people think?

So she stood there, still, a frozen smile fixed on her face, and watched the celebration. All around her, people were laughing, hugging, starting their New Year off right, together.

And still she stood, unseen, unmoving—unloved.

And maybe that was exactly what she deserved.

ROBIN WASSERMAN

Under other circumstances, Kaia supposed she would have enjoyed the little show put on by Haven High's resident star-crossed lovers. But for some reason, she hadn't. Maybe because she hated to see her carefully crafted plans laid to waste, or maybe because her brief alliance with Harper had inspired a twisted kind of loyalty. Maybe it was just because, with two hot guys in her pocket—the sexy prince and the equally sexy pauper—she was feeling unusually charitable. Whatever the reason, she was displeased to see Harper take such a blow—and while Harper had tried her best to play it off, grin and bear it, Kaia wasn't buying. She could see beneath Harper's surface.

And she didn't like what she saw.

She suspected that when she found Adam and Beth—who had quietly and conveniently disappeared—she would like *that* sight even less. Why should Mr. And Mrs. Holier Than Thou get to ride off into the sunset together, no harm, no foul?

Kaia hadn't given anyone any gifts this year. She hadn't felt there was anyone in her life who deserved an act of generosity. But, suddenly, she changed her mind. Harper could use a little pick-me-up—and Kaia knew just what to get her.

This one's for you, Harper, she thought, heading off in search of her prey. *You'd better appreciate it.*

Beth didn't know how much time had passed—a minute, an hour—she knew only that she was back in Adam's arms, and she felt so happy, so safe. She felt like she'd come home. From out here on the front lawn, you could barely hear the party raging inside. It was as if they were all alone. Together.

228

"Well, well, well, so this is what 'happily ever after' looks like."

Beth and Adam sprang apart at the sound of Kaia's caustic voice. Beth glanced over at their unwanted trespasser with disgust, but just smiled tightly and said nothing.

Adam wasn't so polite. "Do you mind?" he snarled. "We're busy."

"So I can see," Kaia said with a smile. "Don't mind me. I just wanted to congratulate the happy couple."

Adam put a possessive arm around Beth and glared at Kaia. "Now you've done it," he said. "So go."

"Okay," she agreed cheerfully. "Good night—and good luck. I hope you actually manage to get her into bed this time."

Beth flinched, but the warm pressure of Adam's hands kept her still.

Ignore her, Beth instructed herself.

"And as for you." Kaia turned to Beth, who steeled herself and promised she wouldn't reward Kaia with a reaction, no matter what the other girl said. "I hope *you'll* be more satisfied by him than I was."

And she walked away.

Adam's face had turned white, all the blood drained away.

"What did she mean by that?" Beth asked, turning to him in hope—and desperation. "What's she talking about?"

Adam was silent. He opened his mouth, but no words came out, and he finally closed it again.

"Adam, what does she *mean*?" Beth asked again, her voice taking on a tinge of panic because, already, she knew.

The look on Adam's face, the look on Kaia's—maybe Beth had always known. Maybe that's why she hadn't asked, hadn't let herself wonder why Kaia had suddenly appeared in—and, just as inexplicably, disappeared from—his life.

"You slept with her, didn't you?" Beth asked harshly, her tone brittle. *She* felt brittle—as if a single touch could shatter her into a million pieces.

He said nothing.

"You slept with her while we were still together," Beth insisted now, with less of a question in her voice.

Still, Adam stood there infuriatingly mute.

"Say something!"

He grabbed her hands, but this time she whipped them away, covering her face. "Just tell me it's not true."

"I can't," he finally admitted.

Her body turned to stone—starting with her heart.

"Beth, can't we just—you said we could make a fresh start—"

"Get away from me," she told him in a husky voice.

"I can't just leave you, not like this," he protested, approaching her. She backed away, almost tumbling backward over the uneven ground.

"I said, get away from me!" She closed her eyes and took a deep breath, trying to stop herself from exploding. Not from yelling or flying at him in a rage, both of which she would have been happy to do if she'd been able, but from literally exploding, from letting the hurt and anger rip her to shreds from the inside out.

"Now, Adam. *Go.*"

And so he did.

Beth stumbled blindly down the long driveway toward

the dark, empty street below. She supposed that she could find someone to give her a ride home, but she preferred to walk. It would take her all night, trudging for miles along the empty highway, but that was all right. She needed the time to think, to plan.

Because this wasn't like before, Beth realized, when Adam had tossed her out with the garbage in what she now realized was a hypocritical fit of jealous rage. She wasn't broken. She wasn't distraught.

She was angry. And the anger made everything clear.

Harper. Kane. Kaia. Adam. They'd all betrayed her. They'd played their little games with her life, kicked her back and forth like a soccer ball, destroyed her, again and again.

So what was she supposed to do now? Go home and cry? Gorge herself on ice cream and whine about how the world was ever so unfair? Blunder through life finding someone else to trust, only to be crushed and stomped on once again?

She didn't think so.

The old Beth might have cried her way home. And, like a nice girl, a good girl, she would have wept, and waited, and wept, until finally, she'd moved on. She'd get past it.

But not this time—not this Beth.

She walked home dry-eyed, her fists clenched, her mind racing.

Because this time, she wasn't going to get past it.

She wasn't going to get over it.

She was going to get even.

Here's a taste of the next *sinful* read . . .

Wrath

It was a mistake.

It had to be.

She'd heard wrong. Or it was a lie.

A dream. A nightmare. Something.

Because if it were true—

If it were true, and this was reality, there was no going back to the person she'd been. Before.

She remembered that person. Hard. Angry. Fury coursing through her veins. It had consumed her, the anger, until her focus narrowed to a single point, a single goal: vengeance.

It had been the perfect plan, every detail seamlessly falling into place. She had lain awake imagining how it would play out, how it would feel to finally take her revenge—wondering whether it would still the voice inside her, the one that howled in pain, that wanted to break something, someone. It was a voice no one else ever heard, ever suspected—but she'd heard, and she'd finally listened. Given in to what it most desired.

Vengeance.

The plan had worked. Everything had unfolded as she'd imagined it. She'd gotten exactly what she'd wanted. But . . .

She'd made a mistake. A fatal error. Because it hadn't gone exactly as planned, had it?

There was supposed to be humiliation—and there was.

There was supposed to be suffering—and there was.

Everything had gone the way it was supposed to. Except—

No one was supposed to die.

Two Weeks Earlier

Beth held herself perfectly still, hoping he would change his mind and disappear. She didn't want to have to speak—and didn't know if she'd be able to force herself to stay silent. Most of all, she didn't want to cry. She didn't want him to know that he could still hurt her; she didn't want him to guess that she stayed up most nights crying. She didn't want him to think that she still cared—because, of course, she did. And more than anything, she wanted to stop.

"Hi," Adam said softly, sliding into the empty seat to her left.

If only the assembly would begin. Then there would be no chance for conversation; Beth could stay silent in the darkness and pretend he wasn't there.

She hadn't looked in his direction yet, but she'd felt him there, hovering, wondering whether or not to sit down. It was as if a part of them was still connected. Not that she would ever acknowledge it; in a just world, any connection between them would have dissolved when he'd slept with Kaia—when he'd broken all the promises between them. When he'd lied about it, when he'd dumped *her* for cheating on *him*, he'd proven how little

Beth meant to him and how little he knew her. She knew all that and could never forget it. So why couldn't she make her body remember? Why couldn't she resist sneaking glances at him out of the corner of her eye, part of her longing to smooth down the windblown tufts of blond hair?

With a few words, she could have him back. "I forgive you." That's all it would take, and she could curl up against him again, his arms warm and strong around her. She could be protected; she could be a "we" again, together, instead of alone.

But she'd promised herself she would never forgive him—*could* never forgive him—and unlike Adam, she kept her promises.

"Beth, you can't ignore me forever," he insisted.

"Watch me." She choked the words out in a whisper. Her lip trembled. *I will* not *cry,* she told herself.

"How many times can I say I'm sorry?" he asked, reaching for her hand. She whipped it away, determined not to let him touch her. She was too angry—and too afraid that if she held his hand or looked in his clear blue eyes, the anger might drain away.

"What do you want from me?" she finally asked. She still couldn't bring herself to look at him. "What do you expect me to say?"

"I don't know. I just . . . I wanted you to know that I'm . . . I mean, if we could just—" He suddenly stopped, and then she did turn to face him. He was doubled over in his seat, head plunged into his hands.

"Just stop," she begged, forcing herself not to lay her hand against his broad back. "Can't we just stop?"

"I can't."

"Why?"

"Because I still love you."

He said it in a pained, strangled voice, without lifting his head. Beth didn't know whether to laugh or cry. Once those words had been able to fix anything; they'd been all she needed to be strong, to be happy, to survive. Now they were miles away from being enough; now they just left her feeling emptier than before.

"I love you," he said again.

And now Beth did something she'd once vowed never to do, not to Adam.

"I don't care."

She lied.

In the old days, Miranda and Harper would have skipped the assembly, taken it as a good excuse to sneak off to the parking lot for a smoke and bitch session about their least favorite people (meaning: 90 percent of the student body).

But these weren't the old days—Miranda wasn't speaking to Harper. Which meant Miranda wasn't speaking to anyone, for it turned out that Harper was the one with all the friends—or at least, followers and hangers on. Miranda, as she'd long suspected, had just been along for the ride.

The ride had made her nauseous one too many times, and she'd finally gotten off. Too bad Harper didn't seem to notice.

"Rand, let's get out of here, what do you say?"

Harper had popped up from behind her seat, and Miranda stifled the impulse to swat her away like a mosquito she'd just caught draining her blood.

"I'd say forget it," she replied wearily, wishing she had the discipline to just keep her mouth shut. The silent treatment had never been her thing. It was hard enough to just stand her ground with Harper—she'd been forgiving her for years, like a bad habit. But this time . . .

All she had to do was picture Kane—his tall, lean body, his knowing grin, his silky voice—and after all those years of dreaming, fantasizing, his image sprung easily to mind. As did the echo of Harper's promise: "You and Kane—it's a done deal. I swear."

And what had Harper done? Pushed him on Beth, all to serve her own dirty, selfish agenda. It was all about Harper. As always.

Harper couldn't even be bothered to deliver a real apology. Sure, she'd groveled for a couple of days, as always, but when Miranda stayed firm, she'd resorted to her standard technique: bravado. It wasn't only ineffective, it was insulting. Miranda could barely stand to watch her, putting on this gruesome show, as if nothing had ever happened, as if things could ever be the same.

"Go find someone else to screw over," Miranda snapped. "I'm done."

"That's great," Harper said. "That's a fabulous way to treat your best friend, you know? What ever happened to forgive and forget?"

"Not my style," Miranda muttered.

"Right, as if you have any style."

Inside, Miranda cringed, and she glanced down at her outfit, a plain white T-shirt and cheap Wal-Mart jeans. Same as yesterday, same as the day before. Five years as sidekick to Haven's alpha girl, and Miranda had somehow remained, to the end, cool by association. And by association only. But Harper had never before flung the bitter truth in her face.

"I'd rather have no style than no class," Miranda replied pointedly. Harper wanted to jab at a soft spot? Two could play that game. And Harper—who still longed for the days when her family had ruled the town, and still chafed at the humiliating turn the Graces had taken, from princely robber baron to penny-pinching dry cleaners—was nothing if not class conscious.

"I have more class—"

"All *you've* got," Miranda interrupted, "is a reputation. And it's about to get worse."

"Is that a threat?" Harper sneered, and for the first time, Miranda knew how it felt to be on the other end of Harper's poisonous gaze of disdain. It hurt. But it only strengthened her resolve. She'd been wondering whether the little revenge plot hatched with Beth was too much, had gone to far—what a waste of worry. Obviously Harper had put their friendship behind her. Miranda could—and would—do the same.

"Give me a break," Harper continued, rolling her eyes. "As if anyone in this school would listen to anything you have to say."

Oh, they would listen.

And then Harper would pay.

"Don't do that, Kane! It tickles!"

Ignoring her pleas—as she intended—Kane picked up the squirmy brunette and hoisted her over his shoulder as she kicked her legs with mock distress.

"Put her down, Kane!" her little friend, a dainty redhead, shrieked. Kane knew it was only because she was eager for her turn.

"Calm down, ladies," he urged them, depositing the brunette back on the ground. He slung an arm around each of them, admiring the way his muscles bulged beneath the tight sleeves of his new Paul Smith shirt. The new weights were working already "You know you love it."

"Whatever," the brunette giggled, shoving him—once their bodies made contact, she didn't pull away.

"Say what you want," he allowed, "but I know you're thrilled to have me back on the market."

The redhead—or more accurately, the *air*head—stood on her toes to give him a kiss on the cheek.

"I just don't know why you stayed away for so long," she whispered, her breath hot against his neck.

Good question.

But he wasn't going to think about that. Those weeks wasted, traipsing around after an ordinary girl, pretending to be something he wasn't, all for . . . for what? It's not like he'd gotten anything out of the deal. Plenty of nagging, and that's about it.

"So what happened?" the brunette asked, tickling the back of his neck. He jerked away. "We thought you were reformed."

"Player no more," her friend chimed in. "Beauty tamed the beast. What gives?"

So what now, the truth?

Right.

Like he'd ever admit that he'd been the one rejected. By a nonentity like Beth. Like he'd ever admit—even to himself—that losing her had cost him something more than his reputation. That it had hurt. Kane never lost; it wasn't his style.

He knew he could turn this around, make it into a win. It would be the easiest thing in the world—a few words and Beth's reputation would be trashed. Kane's would emerge unscathed.

He couldn't do it.

He had no regrets, he insisted to himself. He'd just done what was needed to get what he wanted, same as always. Beth was a big girl, and she'd made her own choices—and, if only briefly, she'd chosen him.

"You can't fool me," she'd said once, kissing him on the cheek. "I know who you really are."

She'd learned how wrong she was, and the lesson had hurt. But Kane couldn't forget that she'd seen something in him, something beyond the smirking mask he showed to the world. And despite everything, he couldn't bring himself to disappoint her yet again.

"Come on, Kane," the redhead pushed. "Dish us some dirt!"

But Kane just smiled mysteriously and tugged her toward him, wishing her hair was blond, her eyes blue and knowing. Wishing she were someone else. "What's the difference what happened?" he asked. "I'm here now—and so are you, which means everyone wins. Right?"

The two girls exchanged a glance, then shrugged.

"We're happy if you're happy," the brunette concluded, rising on her tiptoes to kiss him on the cheek.

Kane forced a grin. He certainly *looked* happy—and isn't that what counts?

✧✧✧

Kaia tipped back her head to catch the last few drops of liquid in the glass, then sucked in an ice cube. She needed something bitingly cool to distract her. Sitting this close to Reed, with a table between them, keeping their bodies apart? It drove her crazy.

"You miss it? Home?"

Kaia opened her mouth to say yes, to give Reed her well-rehearsed speech on the wonders of Manhattan, the sales and the galleries, the way the skyscrapers sliced into the sky on a clear winter morning, to tell him about the late nights, sneaking into club openings and showing up on "Page 6," meeting up at dawn for a goat cheese omelet and bread fresh from the farmer's market before sneaking home to bed. But she stopped before she said anything. If it were anyone else, she wouldn't hesitate, wouldn't admit any wavering in her commitment to her old life, her hatred for the new one. But there was something about Reed that made her want to tell the truth. All of it.

"I don't know," she admitted—and it was the first time she'd let herself think it, much less speak it aloud. Reed didn't say anything, just watched her carefully, let her talk. "Sometimes I do—I hate it here." True. "But . . . I hated it there, too." Also true.

Another guy might have seized the moment, put on the fake sympathy, given her a "comforting" pat on the thigh, and maybe let his hand rest there a bit too long. Shown off his sensitive side. And waited for her to melt into his arms in gratitude.

Not Reed. "What was wrong with it?" he asked.

"I don't know." Kaia sighed. Not a calculated sigh,

designed to elicit pity or to highlight her ample, heaving chest. Just a small, light shiver of air that escaped her as her body sagged with the energy of wondering: What was wrong with her life? "There was my mother. Total bitch. And my—I guess you'd call them my friends." Though they weren't, not really. "But that wasn't it. I just . . ."

And now Reed moved, took her hand—and she knew it wasn't in sympathy or empathy, but out of a desperate need to touch her, because she felt it too.

"I didn't fit there. Not that I fit here," she added, laughing bitterly.

"Know what you mean," Reed said quietly, shaking his head. "But what can you do?"

Kaia didn't say anything, just pressed his hand tightly to her lips. She could never say it out loud, but she knew—bizarrely, she did fit somewhere. Here, with him.

And at least there was some comfort in that.

He had to congratulate himself. He'd made it through the evening without revealing what he suspected, without allowing his emotions to leak through, his anger to explode. She had no idea that he was onto her, that he'd seen her, with *him*.

Hidden in the shadows, he'd watched her betray him. Even then, he couldn't help but admire her delicate porcelain skin, pale as ivory against her ink black hair. She moved like a dancer, every swish of her arm and tilt of her head graceful, deliberate, almost as if she knew he were watching, and was performing just for him. The secretive smile, the way she ran her fingers lightly, softly down her breastbone, pausing at the point where her pendant dropped down into the mysterious darkness between her breasts—he'd pressed against the doorframe to hold himself steady. And for a moment, he'd imagined that his hands followed hers, trailing their way across the soft, creamy skin.

But it was another man who took her hand in his. A stolen hand, a stolen touch—there should be punishment for taking something that doesn't belong to you, he thought now. There should be punishment for giving it away. And yet she did give it away, to the other. Gave her hand freely, wrapped her long slim fingers around his, brought it to her full, red lips.

He could have turned away—he'd seen enough to know the truth. But he had stayed, waited, watched. She could play with all the men she wanted, but in the end, no one knew her like he did. No one but him knew the way she moved when she thought no one was watching.

The time they spent together was poisoned now, tainted with his secret knowledge of what she'd done. But when he watched her in the darkness, that was pure. She could lie to him all she wanted, lie to herself, but he knew the truth: She belonged to him.

Apparently she just needed a reminder.

about the author

Robin Wasserman enjoys writing about high school—but wakes up every day grateful that she doesn't have to relive it. She recently abandoned the beaches and boulevards of Los Angeles for the chilly embrace of the east coast, as all that sun and fun gave her too little to complain about. She now lives and writes in New York City, which she claims to love for its vibrant culture and intellectual life. In reality, she doesn't make it to museums nearly enough, and actually just loves the city for its pizza, its shopping, and the fact that at three a.m. you can always get anything you need— and you can get it delivered.

As many as 1 in 3 Americans
who have HIV... don't know it.

TAKE CONTROL.
KNOW YOUR STATUS.
GET TESTED.

To learn more about HIV testing,
or get a free guide to HIV and
other sexually transmitted diseases:

www.knowhivaids.org
1-866-344-KNOW

Revenge is sweet in a new novel
from the bestselling author
FRANCINE PASCAL

Every high school has its mean girls.
Twyla Gay has had enough—and now she
has a plan. The popular girls' reign of
terror is over. The Ruling Class
is going down.

From Simon Pulse
PUBLISHED BY SIMON & SCHUSTER

A new novel inspired by the explosion of prescription drug abuse among teens

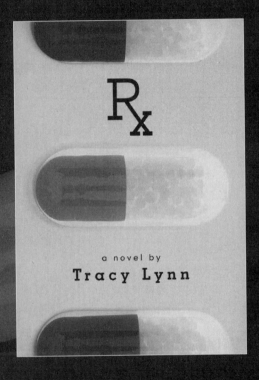

R$_x$

a novel by
Tracy Lynn

GPA, SATs, student council . . .
class superstar Thyme Gilcrest is
dealing with the stress—**by dealing.**

From Simon Pulse
Published by Simon & Schuster